George Watson

Watson's Fifth Book of Reading

SALZWASSER
VERLAG

George Watson

Watson's Fifth Book of Reading

Reprint of the original, first published in 1864.

1st Edition 2022 | ISBN: 978-3-75259-551-2

Verlag (Publisher): Salzwasser Verlag GmbH, Zeilweg 44, 60439 Frankfurt, Deutschland
Vertretungsberechtigt (Authorized to represent): E. Roepke, Zeilweg 44, 60439 Frankfurt, Deutschland
Druck (Print): Books on Demand GmbH, In de Tarpen 42, 22848 Norderstedt, Deutschland

Watson's Educational Series.

WATSON'S

FIFTH BOOK OF READING,

FOR

THE USE OF SCHOOLS.

GLASGOW

MDCCCLXIV.

INTRODUCTORY NOTE.

—o—

In the present Volume, which forms Watson's Fifth Reading Book, it has been the aim of the Publisher, as in all the Reading Books of the Series, to provide the young with volumes adapted not only to impart a knowledge of the mere *art of reading* but to train the pupils to the *love of reading*. Keeping this in view, the Selections to be found in the following pages will no doubt prove both attractive and instructive to the youthful reader.

It has still been thought advisable to put the more difficult words of the Prose Pieces at the head of each, in order that the reading may be facilitated, and these words ought in every case to be carefully gone over before any attempt be made to read the Lesson which follows.

It is hoped that the success and approval which have already attended the other Books of this Series, will be merited by, and extended to, the present effort.

Glasgow, 1864.

CONTENTS.

SECTION I.

SECTION II.

SECTION III.

NATURAL HISTORY.

SECTION IV.

SECTION V.

APPENDIX.

FIFTH BOOK OF READING.

THE HOUR OF PRAYER.

Dis-ci′-ples	For-get′	Be-lieve′
Lis′-ten	Kneel	Suf′-fer
Doubt	Dis-turb′	Thoughts
Tem′-pers	Strength	Friend

Emma and Harry are going to bed. They kneel down at their mother's knee, and say that holy prayer which Jesus made and taught his disciples to use:—"Our Father who art in Heaven."

Their father and mother listen, and lift up their hearts to God, that he too may hear their darlings' voices.

And who will doubt that he listens also. He who when on earth so loved the little children that he called them round him, took them up in his arms and blessed them, will he forget them now he is in heaven? Oh surely not. The little ones now are as dear to him as they were of old. He looks down upon them as they kneel; and let each dear child as it folds its hands and closes its eyes, that the things around may not disturb its thoughts, believe with a glad heart that the blessed Saviour waits to hear its prayer. That from the peaceful blue sky, he sends forth, as if on the wings of an angel, these blessed words, "Suffer little children to come unto me."

Come, then, dear little children, to Jesus, your best friend. Tell him of your sins, your evil tempers, your unkind words. He will forgive you; he shed his blood for you, and he will give you strength to do his will.

Let these thoughts make you love to come before him in your prayers, and then he will so teach you how to pass through the dangers of this world, that you may go at last to dwell with him in heaven.

By the Author of "Early Seeds."

THE LITTLE DROP THAT FELL FROM THE BLACK CLOUD.

Sail'-ing	Sun'-beam	Stream'-lets
Val'-ley	Her'-ald	Foun'-tains
Blos'-som	Liq'-uid	Pre-pare

One summer day, a dark cloud was sailing along through the air, and, because it was alone, it felt very gloomy, and so it burst into tears and wept itself away. And some of its tears fell into the sea, and some upon the rocks; but one little drop went down into a deep valley, and rested upon a broken flower—the last and fairest of its race. It was a lovely blossom, left alone to die in the deep quiet of that shady vale. And when the tear fell upon the flower, it smiled a blessed smile, and felt that it could die in peace, for it was no longer alone; so it closed its soft sweet eye and went to sleep.

Now, close beside the spot where the flower had died, amongst the high green grass, a lark had built her nest; and, just as she stretched her wing to meet the morn, the tear fell upon it from the bosom of the flower.

And so the lark mounted into the air, and began singing to a little sunbeam; and she told it the story of the tear, and of the broken flower. And when the sunbeam heard it, he loved the sweet tear so much, that it kissed it off from the wing of the sweet singer, and took it up to the golden sun: and the sun made it one of his beams, and told it that because it had given comfort to that lovely flower in its dying hour, he would make it his chosen herald,—the first to awake the flowers at morn, and the last to light the bee to her cell at even. And so the tear grew bright, and more bright, until it became a little stream of liquid gold. And every little flower of the earth looked up and loved it, and all the singing birds sang when they beheld it; and the streamlets, and the fountains, and the brooks laughed a joyous laugh when it came down upon their bosoms, and all the earth grew bright with one pure smile.

My little children! do not forget that we are not placed here to do our own work, but the work of Him that made us;—we are not to prepare for this life, but the life which is to come. This little life will soon be past, but there is a country which shall abide forever; a kingdom which knoweth no end, into which, if we have been faithful, we shall one day be taken. There we shall shine brighter than a sunbeam, or the morning star.

"And there we shall hunger no more, neither shall we thirst any more; neither shall the sun light on us, or any heat; for the Lamb which is in the midst of the throne, shall feed us, and shall lead us unto fountains of living waters: and God shall wipe away all tears from our eyes."

Mrs. Jerram.

THE BETTER LAND.

I hear thee speak of the better land;
Thou call'st its children a happy band;
Mother! oh where is that radiant shore.
Shall we not seek it, and weep no more?
Is it where the flower of the orange blows,
And the fire-flies dance through the myrtle boughs?
"Not there, not there, my child!"

Is it where the feathery palm trees rise,
And the date grows ripe under sunny skies?
Or 'midst the green islands of glittering seas,
Where fragrant forests perfume the breeze;
And strange bright birds on their starry wings,
Bear the rich hues of all glorious things?
"Not there, not there, my child!"

Is it far away, in some region old,
Where the rivers wander o'er sands of gold—
Where the burning rays of the ruby shine,
And the diamond lights up the secret mine,
And the pearl gleams forth from the coral strand,
Is it there, sweet mother, that better land?
"Not there, not there, my child!"

Eye hath not seen it, my gentle boy!
Ear hath not heard its deep songs of joy,
Dreams cannot picture a world so fair,
Sorrow and death may not enter there;
Time doth not breathe on its fadeless bloom,
For beyond the clouds, and beyond the tomb,
It is there, it is there, my child!

Mrs. Hemans.

"IT COMES FROM ABOVE."

Or'-phan	Gen'-tle-man	Bir'-ming-ham
Sin'-gu-lar	Re-cov'-ered	Wealth'-y
Pa'-tience	Cir'-cum-stan-ces	Oc-cur'-rence
Prov'-id-ence	Eng'-lish-man	Ben'-e-fit
Prob'-a-bly	Taught	Bus'-i-ness

There was once in France a poor boy, who was called "Little Peter." He was an orphan, and begged his bread from door to door. He sang very prettily, and people seldom sent him away empty-handed. It was an idle and sad life which he led, but Peter had no one to care for him, and he did not know what else to do. He had the singular custom of saying on every occasion, "It comes from above." I will tell you why.

When his father was on his deathbed—if, indeed, he had a bed, for he was very poor—he said to his son, "My dear Peter, you will now be left alone, and many troubles you will have in the world. But always remember, that all comes from above; then you will find it easy to bear everything with patience."

Little Peter understood him, and in order not to forget the words, he often spoke them aloud. He received every gift with the words, "It comes from above." As he grew up, he used to consider what they meant. He was wise enough to see that, as God rules the world, we may well believe of everything that happens in the way of His providence, "It comes from above."

This faith of Little Peter often turned out for his benefit. Once as he was passing through the town, a sudden gust of wind blew off a roof-tile which fell on his shoulder, and struck him to the ground. His first words were, "It comes from above." The bystanders laughed, and thought he must be out of his senses, for of course it could not fall from below; but they did not understand him. A minute after, the wind tore off an entire roof in the same street, which crushed three men to death. Had Little Peter gone on, he would probably have been at that moment just where the roof fell.

Another time, a gentleman employed him to carry a letter to a town, bidding him make all haste. On his way, he tried to spring over a ditch, but it was so wide that he fell in and was nearly drowned. The letter was lost in the mud, and could not be recovered. The gentleman was angry when Little Peter told him of the loss, and drove him out of doors with his whip. "It comes from above," said Peter, as he stood on the steps. The next day the gentleman sent for him. "See here," said he, "there are two half-crowns for you for tumbling into the ditch. Circumstances have now so changed, that it would have been a loss to me had that letter gone safely."

I could tell you much more about Peter. When he had become a big boy, he was still called "Little Peter." A rich gentleman who came into the town, having heard his story, sent for him, in order to give him something. When Little Peter entered the room, the Englishman said, "What think you, Peter; why have I sent for you?" "It comes from above," replied Peter. This answer greatly pleased the gentleman. After thinking a while, he said, "You are right; I will take you into my service, and provide well for you. Will you agree to that?" "It comes from above," answered Peter; "God is very good to me; I will gladly go with you."

So the Englishman took him away. It was a good thing for the poor boy, who had been taught no trade. Long afterwards, we learned that when his master died, he left him a large sum of money to carry on the business; and that "Little Peter" was then a wealthy man in Birmingham. But he still said of every occurrence, "It comes from above."

Dr. Barth.

CHARLES AND JACK.

Be-neath′	Scorn′-ful-ly	Con-fessed′
Sup-port′-ed	Com-pan′-ions	Wick′-ed-ness
Rag′-a-muf-fin	Strug′-gled	Patched
Con-tempt′	Sud′-den	En′-e-my
For-giv′-ing	Oth′-er-wise	Screams

A little boy, whose papa and mamma were very rich, thought it beneath him to speak to a poor boy with patched clothes, who every day passed his father's gate with papers to sell, for this was the way in which he supported himself and his sick mother.

Charles (for that was the rich boy's name) had more than once insulted poor Jack by setting his dog on him, or speaking in a loud tone to his companions about the "little ragamuffin," as he contemptuously styled him. Jack took no notice of all this abuse, for his kind mother had taught him to return good for evil and to love his enemies, because his Saviour commanded him.

Charles was very fond of fishing; he would frequently take his hook and line, and go with some of his companions to a lake about a mile distant. On one occasion of this kind he was seated on the end of a decayed log which projected some distance into the water. A fish played around his hook: he was so intent on catching it that he forgot everything else. Giving the line a sudden jerk, the log tilted, and he was thrown into the deep water. He did not know how to swim, so he struggled about, calling to his companions for aid; but they were all afraid to venture their lives for another. Jack, who was also fishing at a little distance off, hearing the screams of the frightened boys, hastened to know the cause. When he saw Charles struggling and sinking, without once thinking of the evil treatment he had received from him, he plunged into the water and saved his life.

Before Charles had recovered from his wetting, Jack ran off home, not even waiting to receive thanks. The next day Charles sent for him to come to him, as he was quite sick, and therefore not able to go out.

When Jack entered his room, the unhappy boy hung his head; then taking the proferred hand of the poor boy confessed all his past wickedness, asking the forgiveness of him he had once despised.

Never, since then, has Charles spoken in contempt of those whom God has not favoured with riches.

He and Jack are the best of friends; for, says he, "I owe my life to him, how can I be otherwise than grateful?"

Little readers, I hope you may all possess Jack's forgiving spirit. Remember what the Bible says, "If thine enemy hunger, feed him; if he thirst, give him drink."

American Visitor.

THE CHILD AND THE STAR.

" They tell me, dear father, each gem in the sky,
That sparkles at night is a star:
But *why* do they dwell in those regions so high,
And shed their cold lustre so far?
I *know* that the sun makes the blossoms to spring,
That it gives to the flow'rets their birth,
But *what* are the stars? do they nothing but fling
Their cold rays of light upon earth?"

" My child, it is said, that yon stars in the sky,
Are worlds that are fashioned like this,
Where the souls of the good and the gentle, who die,
Assemble together in bliss;

And the rays that they shed o'er the earth is the light
Of His glory, whose throne is above,
That tell us, who dwell in these regions of night,
How great is His goodness and love."

"Then, father, why still press your hand to your brow,
Why still are your cheeks pale with care?
If all that was gentle be dwelling there now,
Dear mother, I know, must be there."
"Thou chidest me well," said the father, with pain,
"Thy wisdom is greater, by far;
We may mourn for the lost, but we should not complain,
While we gaze on each beautiful star."

J. E. Carpenter.

THE CLOUDS.

Sul'-try	Mead'-ows	A-maze'-ment
Cab'-bage	Joy'-ful-ly	Ex-traor'-di-na-ry
Cur'-tains	Grat'-i-tude	Pur'-ple
En-grav'-ings	Beau'-ti-ful	Po-ta'-toes

One day John and Mary took a walk with their father. It was a very warm, sultry day, and far up in the sky were many clouds.

"Just look, Papa," said John, "what big clouds!"

"Oh yes," said Mary, "I wonder what the Lord has made the clouds for?"

"The clouds are very useful," said the father; "the Lord has made them because He loves us. The clouds are big *curtains*."

"Curtains?" exclaimed the children astonished.

"Yes, truly," answered the father; "don't you know what we use curtains for?"

"Oh yes," said Mary; "I know. When the sun

shines too strongly, we pull down the curtains to keep off the heat."

"Quite so," replied the father. "Now, when the sun shines very hot on the fields, the cows in the meadows are sadly annoyed, and the flowers and plants bow their little heads to the ground. Then the Lord spreads out the clouds before the sun, just as you pull down the curtains, and the cows begin to leap and to run about joyfully, and the flowers and plants lift up their heads with gratitude."

While the father was speaking it began to rain. They went into a farm-house for shelter. The children placed themselves at the window to look at the rain, which was falling in heavy showers.

"That rain, too," said the father, "comes from the clouds."

"What a pity!" said John, "we can't walk now; everything is wet."

"True," answered the father; "still it is very useful. The Lord has made the clouds to give rain; they are big *watering-pots.*"

"Watering-pots?" said Mary with amazement.

"Yes, my dear," said the father. "What does our gardener use his watering-pot for?"

"To wet the ground," said John, quickly.

"Yes," continued Mary, "for if the ground is too dry the flowers will not grow."

"Just so," said the father; "but when the big meadows and fields are too dry, who is the Great Gardener who is able to water them? And when the farmer's land is so dry, that the potatoes, and the cabbage, and the wheat won't grow, who is to wet all that?"

"Oh! I see! I see!" exclaimed John. "Then the Lord takes those big clouds and presses rain out of them."

"He does," said the father. "The clouds are big watering-pots with which the Lord wets this beautiful earth of ours, just as the gardener wets our garden."

The rain was soon over, and the father again went out with his children.

"How nice it is!" they said, as they inhaled the cool, fresh air.

"Ay," said the father, "the Lord has done it with his big watering-pots. Now, look at the clouds!"

The children looked up and clapped their hands.

"Oh!" they cried, "how beautiful!"

Here the great clouds floated about in the sky. The sun had just broken through them, and given them all sorts of fine colours. Some had gilt edges; others were red like crimson; some again were purple, pink, light-blue, and dark-blue. Many of them, too, had most extraordinary forms. On the left-hand side was a large bluish cloud that looked like a large ship, with its sails set up to the top. On the right was a dark cloud, that had very much the shape of a big cow with three horns.

The children looked with delight at the beautiful sights above them.

"Now, you see," said the father, "that the clouds are *pictures* too. We hang up pictures and engravings in our rooms: so, the Lord hangs up golden, purple, and blue clouds on the walls of the sky, to make a beautiful drawing-room of our whole earth."

Dr. Liefde.

——o——

LITTLE DICK AND THE GIANT.

Whis'-tling	Fright'-ened	Wretch'-ed
Thirst'-y	Vic'-tims	I'-ron
Hun'-dred	Pris'-on	Gi'-ant
Laughed	Din'-ner	An'-gry
Mo'-ment	Crammed	Strug'-gled

Little Dick, what a gay fellow he was! He used to go singing and whistling about the whole day long. He was always merry, and scarcely anything could make him sad. One day, little Dick thought he would have a ramble in the forest, at some distance from his home. So off he set in high spirits, singing and whistling, till he made the woods ring again.

At last he reached a clear brook that ran through the wood; and being thirsty, he stooped down to drink. But just at that moment he was suddenly seized from behind, and found himself in the hands of a great, tall giant, a hundred times as big as himself. The giant looked at him with great delight, and then put him into a large bag, and carried him off.

Poor Dicky tried all he could to get out of the bag, but to no purpose. He screamed, he struggled, he tried to tear the bag, but the giant only laughed at him for his pains, and went on, holding him fast.

At last the giant came to his house,—a gloomy-looking place, with a high wall all round it, and no trees or flowers. When he got in, he shut the door, and took Dicky out of the bag. The poor captive now thought his time was come; for when he looked round he saw a large fire, and before it two victims larger than himself roasting for the giant's dinner. The giant, however, did not kill Dick, but only put him into a prison which he had prepared for him. It was quite dark, with cross-bars all round it; and the only food in it was a piece of dry bread and a cup of water. Dick beat his head against the iron bars, and dashed backwards and forwards, and felt very wretched.

The next day the giant came and looked at Dick; and, finding that he had eaten none of the bread, he took him by the head, and crammed some of it down his throat. Poor Dick was too much frightened to think of eating or drinking.

He was left all alone in the dark another day, and a sad day it was. The poor creature thought of his own home, his companions, the sun-light, the trees, the flowers, and the many nice things he used to eat; and then he screamed, and tried to get between the bars, and beat and tore himself.

The giant came again, and wanted Dick to sing as he used to do, and be happy and merry. " Sing, sing, sing!" said he; but Dick was much too sad to sing. A prison is no place to sing songs in. At last the giant grew angry, and took Dick out to force him to sing. Dick gave a loud scream, plunged, and struggled, and then sank dead in the giant's hand!

This is a true story.—Poor Dicky was a *little bird*, and that giant was a *cruel boy*.

The Youth's Friend.

THE OAK TREE.

The oak tree was an acorn once,
  And fell upon the earth;
And sun and showers nourished it,
  And gave the oak tree birth.

The little sprouting oak tree!
  Two leaves it had at first,
Till sun and showers nourished it,
  Then out the branches burst.

The little sapling oak tree!
 Its root was like a thread,
Till the kindly earth had nourished it,
 Then out it freely spread.

On this side and on that
 It grappled with the ground,
And in the ancient rifted rock
 Its firmest footing found.

The winds came, and the rains fell;
 The gusty tempests blew;
All, all were friends to the oak tree,
 And stronger yet it grew.

The boy that saw the acorn fall,
 He feeble grew and gray;
But the oak was still a thriving tree,
 And strengthened every day.

Four centuries grows the oak tree,
 Nor does its verdure fail;
Its heart is like the iron wood,
 Its bark the plaited mail.

Now cut us down the oak tree,
 The monarch of the wood,
And of its timber stout and strong
 We 'll build a vessel good.

The oak tree of the forest
 Both east and west shall fly,
And the blessings of far distant lands
 Upon our ship shall lie.

For she shall not be a man-of-war,
 Nor a pirate shall she be,
But a noble Christian merchant ship,
 To sail upon the sea.

Mrs. Howitt.

THE FRETFUL FIR.—Part I.

Cap′-i-tal	Ceil′-ing	Shud′-der	State′-ly
Val′-ue	Wag′-gon	Christ′-mas	Ex-pec-ta′-tion
Sur′-vey	Swal′-lows	Cher′-uped	Im-me′-di-ate-ly
Au′-tumn	Hith′-er	Com-pan′-ions	Or′-na-ment
Wal′-nuts	E′-gypt	Com′-fort-a-ble	En-twined′

A pretty little fir-tree once stood in the forest. It had a capital place, which was open to the sunshine and the air, and around it grew many of its taller brothers. But none of these things had any value in the eyes of the little fir tree—it only wished to grow tall. "O that I were a tall tree," it said; "then I should be able to stretch my branches out so far, and lift my head so high, as to take a survey of the wide world around me."

In the autumn, wood-cutters came and felled some of the largest trees; and the young fir, which had now grown to a good height, felt a shudder; for the stately trees fell crashing to the earth; their boughs were hewn away; and they were put upon drays and dragged out of the wood. "Where can they be going to?" thought the little fir-tree.

In the spring, when the storks and swallows came, the little fir-tree said to them, "Did you meet the tall firs on the way?" "I met," replied the stork, "a great number of ships as I flew hither from Egypt; in these ships there were stately masts; and I will be bound they were the firs, for they had the smell of firs about them." "Oh, if I were but tall enough to sail across the sea!" said the little fir-tree.

When Christmas drew near, quite young trees were cut down—trees that were neither so tall nor so old as this fretful fir-tree, that was always wishing to be off. These young trees were laid on waggons with all their branches on, and drawn away out of the wood. "Where can they be going to?" said the fir-tree. "We know, we know," cheruped the sparrows: "we have peeped in at the windows, and seen young trees planted straight upright in the middle of nice warm rooms, and tricked out with such fine things—apples, nuts, pretty toys, and hundreds of candles." "That is better than sailing across the sea," shouted the joyful fir-tree; "how I long to be among them! oh, to think of being in the waggon, and then in the warm room, with all those fine things hanging on one; and there must be something better after all than that, or else why should they deck one out so?"

The little fir-tree grew taller and taller, and next year, at Christmas-time, it was cut down the first of all. The axe cut through to the marrow, and the tree fell to the earth with a sigh. It felt a pain and faintness—it could not think of being happy then. It felt sad, too, at parting from its home—the spot where it had shot up so fairly; and it feared it would never see its old companions again, the little bushes and flowers around it, perhaps not even the birds.

The journey on the waggon had nothing comfortable about it; nor did the little fir-tree come properly to itself, till after being taken out of the cart, it heard a man say, "This is a beautiful one; this will do." It was now carried into a fine drawing-room, and placed in a large tub filled with sand; but no one could see that it was a tub, for it was hung all round with green twigs, and was standing on a gay carpet. Oh, how the tree trembled with expectation! Immediately both the servants and the ladies began to ornament it. They stuck apples and walnuts upon it; and above a hundred red, blue, and white little candles were fastened to its branches. Dolls, too, and other toys were entwined with the green; and at the top of all shone a spangled gold star. Next the candles were lighted—and how bright, how beautiful it was! The tree trembled in all its branches with joy.

But, behold, the folding doors were thrown open, and a troop of children rushed in. They danced round the tree, and shouted, till the lights burned down to the branches, and were put out. Then, having leave to plunder the tree, they rushed wildly at it, till all its branches cracked again; and if it had not been fastened to the ceiling by the gold star at the top of it, it must certainly have been thrown down. At last the children became weary of their sport, and retired for the night; and no one thought about the tree, except the old nurse who came and peeped among the branches to see if a fig or apple had not been forgotten.

Hans Andersen.

THE FRETFUL FIR—PART II.

Gar'-ret	Dis'-mal	Dan'-gled
Pan'-try	Tal'-low	Pres'-ent-ly
Hang'-ing	Ba'-con	Trel'-lis
Stu'-pid	Pris'-o-ner	Per-fume'
Ter'-ri-bly	Rights	Sigh'-ing

In the morning the footman and the housemaid came into the drawing-room. "Now," thought the tree, "my fine dress is going to be put on again." But they dragged it out of the room, up the stairs, to the garret-floor, and there they placed it in a dark corner where the daylight never shone. "What can this mean? what am I to do here?" thought the tree; and it leaned against the wall thinking and thinking. Time enough it had to do so, for days and weeks passed, and yet no one came near it. "It must be winter now," thought the tree; "the earth is hard and covered with snow, men cannot plant me; so most likely I am to stay here under shelter till the spring comes: how well-advised that is! how good men are!—though I wish it were not quite so dark and dismal here."

"Pip, pip," said a little mouse, as he popped out of his hole, and snuffed at the fir tree: "Can you tell me how to get to the pantry where cheese lies on the shelves, and hams are hanging from the ceiling, where you can go in lean, and come out fat? Can you tell me this, you old fir-tree?" "I am not old," said the fir-tree; "nor do I know anything about the pantry; but I know the wood very well, where the sun shines, and the little birds sing." "You are a stupid old tree," said the little mouse, and went back to its hole.

The next night two rats came. We are terribly hungry," said the rats; "do you know where we shall find bacon or tallow-candles, you old fir-tree?" "I am not old," said the tree; "and I never saw bacon." "Then good luck to you," replied the rats; and so saying they went back to their friends.

But the fir-tree was not to be always a prisoner. One morning people came to set things to rights in the garret; and finding the tree there, they pulled it out, and dragged it down stairs into the daylight. "Now life begins again," thought the tree, for it felt the fresh air and the first beams of the sun. Presently it was in the yard again. The yard was close to a garden, where everything was in bloom. The roses hung over the light trellis-work, full of freshness and perfume; the linden-trees were in blossom; and the swallows flew about singing "Quirre-virrart." "Now I shall begin life again," cried the fir-tree; and it stretched out its branches. But, alas! they were all dry and yellow, though the gold-paper star still dangled at its top, and glittered in the sunshine.

Some of the merry-hearted children who had danced round the tree at Christmas, were playing in the yard.

One of them ran and tore off the gold star. "Just look what was hanging on the ugly old fir-tree," said he: and he trampled on the branches till they cracked again. Then the tree saw the flowers in the garden in all the freshness of their beauty, and then it looked at itself and wished that it had never left the green forest.

Soon after the man-servant came and cut up the tree into little pieces, and carried a whole bundle of it into the brew-house. It blazed up brightly under the large brewing-copper, sighing and cracking as it blazed. The children ran in and looked at the fire, crying "Pop! bang!" while, at every crack, the fir-tree thought sorrowfully of the summer days in the wood, and of the winter nights when the stars were twinkling. And then it was all burnt to ashes.

Ibid.

CHARLIE AND THE ROBIN'S SONG.

Char'-lie	Clear'-er	Whis'-per
Rob'-in	Crav'-ing	Trill'-ing
Pray'-ing	Chirp'-ing	Bird'-lings

One summer morning early.
  When the dew was bright to see,
Our dark-eyed little Charlie
  Stood by his mother's knee.
And he heard a robin singing,
  In a tree so tall and high,
On the topmost bough 'twas swinging,
  Away up in the sky.

"Mamma, the robin's praying,
  In the very tree-top there;
Glory! glory! it is saying,
  And that is all its prayer.

But God will surely hear him,
  And the angels standing by,
For God is very near him,
  Away up in the sky."

"My child! God is no nearer
  To robin on the tree,
And does not hear him clearer
  Than he does you and me.
For he hears the angels harping,
  In sun-bright glory drest,
And the little birdlings chirping
  Down in their leafy nest."

"Mamma, if you should hide me
  Away down in the dark,
And leave no lamp beside me,
  Would God then have to hark?
And if I whisper lowly,
  All covered in my bed,
Do you think that Jesus holy
  Would know what 'twas I said?"

"My darling little lisper,
  God's light is never dim;
*The very lowest whisper
  Is always close to him.*"

Now, the robin's song was filling
  The child's soul full of bliss;
The very air was trilling
  When his mamma told him this.
And he wished, in childish craving,
  For the robin's wings to fly,
To sing on tree-tops waving,
  So very near the sky.

Child at Home.

CHARLIE AND HIS DOG.

Fa'-vour-ite	Im-per'-ti-nent	Ad'-mi-ral
Con'-stant	Col'-lar	Of-fend'-ed
Com-pan-'ion	Suc-ces'-sion	Tem'-pers
Re-spect'-a-ble	Dog'-gie	A-cross'

Some years since, a little boy named Charlie had a large favourite dog, that was his constant companion in playhours. This dog, whom we shall call Rover, was a fine respectable-looking animal, with one of the best of tempers. He never quarrelled with other dogs, and would let the merry, impertinent little Carlo frisk about his heels, without being in the least offended. How I wish all *boys* were like him in this respect.

Rover was very fond of the water, and in hot weather he used to swim across the river near which Charlie lived. One day Charlie tied a string to his dog's collar, and ran down with him to the water's edge. Then he took off his clothes, and holding hard by the dog's neck and the bit of string, he went into the river, and Rover pulled across. After playing about on the other side, they returned in the way they had come; but when Charlie looked for his clothes, he could find nothing but his shoes, the wind had blown all the rest into the water.

Rover saw what had happened, and making his little master let go the string, he dashed into the river, and first brought out his coat, and then all the rest in succession. Charlie dressed, and went home in his wet things, and told his mother what fun he and Rover had had. His mother told him that he had done very wrong in going across the river as he had done, and that he should thank God for making the dog take him over and back again safely; for if Rover had made him let go in the river, he would most likely have sunk, and been drowned.

"Shall I thank God now, mamma?" said little Charlie, and he kneeled down at his mother's knee, and thanked God. Then, getting up again, he threw his arms around Rover's neck, saying, "I thank you too, dear doggie, for not letting go."

"Little Charlie," lived to grow up to be a man, and afterwards became Admiral Sir Charles Napier.

Sunday Scholar's Magazine.

THE GLUTTONOUS BEAR.—A FABLE.

A-poth'-e-ca-ry	Liqu'-or	Re-lief'
Poi'-son-ous	Med'-i-cine	Rē-mem'-ber
Ar'-ti-cles	Per-spi-ra'-tion	Snor'-ing
Cap'-i-tal	Di-rec'-tions	Com'-pass

There was a bear who was very fond of dainties and sweetmeats. Once upon a time he stole at evening into an apothecary's cellar. There were a great many pots, basins, and barrels filled with sweet and sour, and poisonous articles.

"Capital!" said he, with a whispering voice. "Here is plenty of dainties. Now for a feast!"

He put his nose into the first barrel that presented itself, and smelled the liquor which it contained.

"Brr!" he said, shaking his head too and fro. "This smells like soot from the chimney; but here is a pot with a fine yellow jelly—I wonder how it smells."

He put his nose to the pot, and was delighted with the smell. Now, that jelly was a very strong and sickening medicine. He snuffed at the pot, inside and outside.

"That's it!" he said; "that's the thing for me!"

He pushed out his tongue, and began licking, and he *kept* on licking till he had swallowed the whole contents. He then sneaked away to the forest, and laid himself down in his den."

It was not long, however, before Mr. Bruin became so sick that he could not lift up his eyelids. The perspiration broke out all over his body. He stretched himself out at full length, with his legs in all the directions of the compass, and beat the ground with his tail, as if he were threshing corn. "Boo! baa!" he groaned; "what ails me? O dear! I'm choking! I'll vomit my heart out of my body! Woe's me! I'll never touch a pot again; no, never; never, I say, in all my life;—never!"

Thus he groaned and roared, till the forest resounded. At length he got some relief, and when he felt a little better, he said to himself,—"Dear me, that was a job; I thought I had swallowed the whole sea, together with the moon and stars. Whatever I may or may not do, I'll never taste dainties again."

He thereupon laid himself on his side. and fell asleep, snoring as loudly as a bear can snore.

The next evening Mr. Bruin once more went out a-hunting. He passed by the apothecary's cellar.

"No, no," said he; "I wont go in. I'll take care this time; never such a thing again;—never in my life."

So he passed on. But soon he stopped, and, looking back at the cellar, he said—

"I remember there were some very nice-looking pots. I wonder what they contain. Of course I wont taste anything; but I might take a smell—only a smell."

So he returned to the cellar, and began snuffing at the pots. At length he stopped at one that smelled very nicely.

"I'm sure," he said, "that's something very fine. I don't think I ever smelt anything so sweet in my life. Just let me take one drop—only one single drop."

He pushed out his tongue and tasted. It was a strong poison, but sweet as honey. He tasted again—again—again; and then fell down—dead as a door nail.

De. Liefde.

LITTLE BIRD WITH BOSOM RED.

Little bird, with bosom red,
Welcome to my humble shed!
Daily near my table steal
While I pick my scanty meal.
Doubt not, little though there be,
But I'll cast a crumb to thee;
Well rewarded if I spy
Pleasure glancing in thine eye.

See thee, when thou 'st ate thy fill,
Plume thy breast and wipe thy bill,
Pouring forth thy grateful note,
Innocent as sweet thy throat!
Come my feather'd friend again,
Well thou know'st the broken pane;
Ask of me thy daily store,
Ever welcome to my door.

Langhorne.

THE FOX, THE GOAT, AND THE CARROTS.

A FABLE.

Car'-rots	Re-bound'-ed	Treas'-ure
Cour'-age	Tri'-fle	Quar'-rel
Im-mov'-a-ble	Hol-loa'	Peas'-ant
Vi'-o-lent-ly	Coun'-te-nance	Ma-li'-cious-ly

A Fox and a goat were walking together on the main road. After having advanced a few yards, they saw a bag lying at the side of the hedge.

"I wonder what there may be in that bag." said the goat.

"I'll see," said the fox; and, putting his mouth to the string with which the bag was tied, he bit it through in a moment; then seizing the bottom of the bag with his teeth, he shook it, and the most splendid carrots rolled out.

"Those are for me," said the fox, "for I have opened the bag."

"You shan't touch them," answered the goat, "else I'll batter you with my horns, till your ribs crack."

The fox looked at the large horns of the goat, and showed his teeth. The goat, seeing the fox's teeth, thought within himself, "I don't like those sharp fellows." And the fox thought, "I don't believe my ribs would stand those horns."

So they kept standing over the carrots, and looked at each other, but neither had the courage to touch the spoil.

After a pause the fox said, "What's the use of our standing here? Let us see which of us is the stronger. Yonder are two heaps of stones; take you one of them and I'll take the other. He who first throws down his heap shall have the carrots."

"Very well," said the goat. So they went each to his heap.

The goat placed himself on his hind legs, and knocked with his horns till the ground rebounded, but the heap kept immovable.

"You don't hit hard enough," said the fox; "take a run at it."

The goat went a few steps back, and ran at the heap as violently as he could. Crack! crack! and both his horns fell down to the ground.

When the fox saw this, he began dancing on his hind legs.

"Ah! my dear fellow," cried he, "the carrots are now for me."

"Not yet," said the goat. "You haven't thrown down your heap. And if you touch the carrots before then, I'll fight you with the stumps that are left on my head."

The fox looked at the goat's stumps, and thought one of them is very sharp; he might rip up my sides. "Very well," said he; "I'll throw down my heap; it's a trifle to me."

The fox began digging round with his fore-feet till there was a large hole in the ground; but, holloa! it fell on the fox and broke his left hind leg.

There they stood looking at one another with a sad countenance, the one with broken horns, and the other with a broken leg.

"Jump at the carrots!" said the goat maliciously. "I now leave them to you."

"I can't," sighed the fox, "my leg pains me too much. You may take them."

"Very well," said the goat, and ran towards the bag. But, oh, dear! there was neither bag nor carrots; for, during their quarrel, a peasant had passed by and picked up both.

"Alas!" cried the goat, "what fools we are! Had we divided the treasure in peace, I would have saved my horns, you your leg, and each of us would have had enough of carrots."

De Liefde.

THE MATCHES.

Flour'-ish-ing	A-sun'-der	Im-me'-di-ate-ly
Beau'-ti-ful	As-signed'	Deign
Ward'-robe	Clois'-ter	Jeal'-ous-ies
Splen'-did	Yes'-ter-day	Vul'-gar

There was once a bundle of Matches that could not contain themselves for pride, because they thought they were of such high birth. Their father, the fir, had in olden times been a great tall tree in one of the northern forests. But these Matches were now lying beside a kitchen grate, between a tinder-box and an old iron pot, to which they told most wonderful stories about their younger days. "Yes, when we were on the green bough," said they, "then we really had a flourishing time of it. All the day long we had sunshine, and the little birds amused us with merry songs. We could see plainly enough, too, that we were rich; for while other trees put on a decent dress only in summer, our family had its beautiful green wardrobe all the year. At last in the midst of this happy kind of life, the wood-cutters came; and this was what split our family asunder. Our mighty father got a place as mainmast to a splendid ship, which could sail round the world. The other branches of the family went somewhere else. And to *us* was assigned the office of making a light for the common throng."

"The rest of us are probably as well born as you," replied the Iron Pot; "but what does our high birth avail us in this dull place. Excepting the Water Can, which sometimes goes down into the yard, we live more retired here than in a cloister. Our only news-bearer is the Market Basket; but he makes such a chatter about what he hears and sees, that only yesterday an old pot fell down and broke in two, in sheer alarm at his noise."

"Have done with your nonsense about birth," said the Tinder-box, putting in a word; "let us have some sport while the housemaid is in bed." And immediately Flint and Steel struck so hard against each other that they sparkled, as if to say, "What a merry night we shall have of it!"

"Let us talk about who is the grandest of us all," said the Matches.

"No, I will have a dance," said the Fire-tongs; and

away it danced, throwing up into the air first the one leg and then the other. Oh, what a sight to be sure! The old Chair-cover in the corner burst with laughter at the very sight of it.

"Pooh, how very vulgar!" thought the Matches.

Then the Tea-urn was called on for a song. But she said she had a cold, and could only sing when she was boiling. But the fact was, she would not deign to sing till she found herself among the great folks in the drawing-room.

"If the Tea-urn will not sing, I will," said the Tea-kettle, who was chief kitchen-singer, and half-brother to the former.

"No jealousies," said the Market-basket: "is this the way to pass the night? Would it not be much better to turn the house topsy-turvy? then each would get into his right place. That would be something like fun to us."

"Yes, let us make a regular to-do," cried they all with one voice.

At this moment the door opened. It was the housemaid; and Pot, Pan, Kettle, and Tea-urn were still in a moment. The housemaid took the Matches, and made a light with them. Oh, how they crackled and burned in the yellow-blue flame!

"Now then," thought they, "every blockhead must see that we stand first, and how brightly we shine;" and so saying they were burned to ashes.

Hans Andersen.

CHILD'S EVENING PRAYER.

Ere on my bed my limbs I lay,
God grant me grace my prayers to say.
O God, preserve my mother dear
In health and strength for many a year;

And, Oh, preserve my father too,
And may I pay him reverence due;
And may I my best thoughts employ
To be my parents' hope and joy!
My sisters and my brothers both,
From evil guard, and save from sloth,
And may we always love each other,
Our friends, our father, and our mother!
And still, O Lord, to me impart
A contrite, pure, and grateful heart,
That after my last sleep I may
Awake to thy eternal day. Amen.

Coleridge.

"WORK."—Part I.

Guess	His'-to-ry	Spec'-ta-cle
Gram'-mar	Ob-jec'-tion	Yawn
A-rith'-me-tic	Ig'-nor-ant	Sulk'-y
Prac'-tis-ing	Mis'-er-a-ble	Stitch
Pi-a'-no	Pun'-ish-ment	Sheaves

My young readers, whether would you rather play or work? I think I can guess your answer—"Play, play, play." Is it not? Well, I don't blame you for liking your play; but what say you about work as well as play? Do you like it also? "No," says Tom; "I don't like these lessons about grammar." "Nor I," says Jack, "this arithmetic." "Nor I," says Jane, this practising on the piano to learn music, or this stitch, stitch, stitching, to learn to sew." "Nor I," says Mary, "this French lesson, and these long pages of history." But you would all like to play, would you not? And to laugh, romp, sing, swing, and amuse yourselves all day long? No lessons to learn, no one to find fault, no one to trouble you,—but just to enjoy yourselves in being idle, and doing whatever you pleased?

Now, I know your parents and masters have no objection that you should have your nice and happy games, because they love you; but for the very same reason they will make you work, whether you like it or not. They know that, if you were allowed to grow up idle and ignorant, you would be both useless and miserable. But would it not be better, my young friends, if you liked your work, and did it with a good-will? And why? Just because it is *right:* for it is given you by God, your Master and your Father, who also gives you all your play and enjoyment. Now, it is a delightful sight to see you enjoy your play heartily; but Oh! it is an ugly sight to see a boy or girl idle and lazy, hating their duty—to see them dragged to their lessons, as if it were a punishment—to see them sulky or sleepy over them, as if they said, "Although it is all for our good, and although it pleases our parents and masters on earth, and our Father and Master in heaven, when we do our duty carefully and cheerfully, yet we hate it, and won't do it if we can help it." I say again, that a lazy boy or girl is a sad spectacle, and no one can love or respect them, for they are selfish, disobedient, and useless.

Come and learn a lesson from the ploughman in the field. See how he bends his neck to his work, and how, with strong arms and steady eye, he guides his plough along the furrow. See these noble horses how they press forward, and put their whole strength to the plough, so that it moves on without a halt, and turns up the earth like brown waves. Look, too, at these wild sea-gulls that have left the white waves of that ocean which is breaking on the shore, and have fled far to gather their day's food from the dark waves of this furrowed field. See the black rooks that have come from their trees to join their white friends from the ocean, and are getting such a dinner as they have not tasted during the whole winter. How busy they all are! There is no idleness or laziness here. And what would become of us if every one was to become idle and sulky, and yawn, and get cross, and say, "Oh I don't like work; I won't do it; I want fun, and nothing but fun." Well, let us see how you would get on if everybody took this into their head.

You want shoes. "Oh!" says every shoemaker, "we don't like working and we won't make shoes; these children may go bare-footed." You want clothes. "Oh!" says every tailor, "we don't like work, and we won't cut clothes or stitch them; these children may go naked." You want a house. "Oh!" says every mason, "we don't like work, and we won't build a house; these children may lie in the fields." You want bread. "I won't work," says the baker. "Then give us the flour," you cry. "I won't work and grind it," says the miller. "Then give us the wheat." "I wont work and thrash it," says the farmer. "Then give us the sheaves." "We won't work and cut them down," say the reapers. "Oh, then, do get another field, and sow some wheat for us, or we shall die of starvation," cry the children. But neither the ploughman nor horses will work. They all wish to be idle, and to amuse themselves. What, now, is to become of us if every one resolves to be idle? Oh! children, I daresay you smile when you think how all the world would suffer and die if all became lazy, like some boys and girls I have seen, who say,—"We don't like work, and we won't do it."

Good Words.

"WORK."—PART II.

Cir'-cuits	Ex-am'-ple	Sav'-iour
Slug'-gard	Re-mem'-ber	Con-tin'-u-al-ly
Shep'-herd	Pa'-tri-archs	Car'-pen-ter
A-pos'-tle	Faith'-ful	Pov'-er-ty

My dear children, it is God's will that we should work. See how He works Himself. He has made everything you see on earth, and in the sky; and it is He who takes care of all. See, too, how He has made everything to be useful, and nothing to be idle, and to live for itself alone. The sun is giving its heat and light to the world, and the clouds carry water and pour it in showers over the earth, and the earth brings forth its food for man and beast. "The sun also ariseth, and the sun goeth down, and hasteth to his place where he arose. The wind goeth toward the south, and turneth about unto the north; it whirleth about continually; and the wind returneth again according to his circuits. All the rivers run into the sea; yet the sea is not full: unto the place from whence the rivers come, thither they return again. All things are full of labour." (Eccles. i., 5-8.) Every beast, and bird, and insect, too, is busy all the day, and some at night, in providing food for themselves or their young, or in making houses or nests for themselves. This is what God says to the lazy:—"Go to the ant, thou sluggard; consider her ways, and be wise: which having no guide, overseer, or ruler, provideth her meat in the summer, and gathereth her food in the harvest. How long wilt thou sleep, O sluggard? when wilt thou arise out of thy sleep? Yet a little sleep, a little slumber, a little folding of the hands to sleep: so shall thy poverty come as one that travelleth, and thy want as an armed man." (Proverbs vi., 6-11.)

And all the good people about whom you read in the Bible were busy and active in their work. Abraham, Isaac, and Jacob travelled far, and worked hard as shepherds. Joseph was one of the busiest men in Egypt. Moses worked till he was one hundred and twenty years old. The Apostle Paul travelled and preached for thirty years, and supported himself and others by the labour of his hands, and it was he who said, that "If any man did not work, neither let him eat."

But why need I mention any other example, when we have the life of God's dear Son, our Saviour, Jesus Christ. He worked with his own hands as a carpenter, at Nazareth. When He began to preach He went about doing good, night and day, labouring for others; often wearied, but never slothful. It was He who said, "I must work the work of Him that sent me while it is called to-day." And ere He left the world He said,—"I have finished the work Thou hast given me to do."

Dear children, we must learn to have the same spirit if we wish to be friends of Christ, and children of God. Remember, too, that we must give an account at the great day of judgment, of the way in which we live now. Boys and girls can know their duties just as well as other people, and they can please God just as well as the patriarchs and apostles, by doing what is right as they did. If you are thus faithful, when young, over a few small things, like learning lessons, or doing whatever work is your duty, your Master in heaven will be able to say to you,—"Well done, good and faithful servant: thou hast been faithful over a few things, I will make thee ruler over many things." But the same Master will, in anger, say to a lazy and unfaithful boy or girl,—"O thou wicked and slothful servant!" Pray to God, then, to bless you every day, to do your work honestly, cheerfully, and well, and then you will enjoy your play the more, for you will be happy in your own heart, and pleased with yourselves, because you have tried to please God. *Ibid.*

THE STINGING NETTLE.

Blis'-ters	A-light'-ed	Whole'-some
Beau'-ti-ful	Sat'-is-fied	Tres'-pass
Tin'-gle	Char'-ac-ter	Ex-am'-in-ing
Ter'-ri-bly	Ex'-cel-lent	Con'-se-quenc-es
Por'-ridge	Bus'-iness	In-struc'-tion

Alfred saw a beautiful flower growing on the other side of a deep ditch; and he ran forward to get it for his sister Mary. Mary begged him not to do so, lest he should tumble into the ditch. But Alfred would have his own way. As he was getting down the bank his foot slipped; and he would have fallen into the ditch, had he not caught hold of some nettles which grew on the bank. He was not long in getting up the bank again; for the sharp sting of the nettles made him forget the beautiful flower.

"There now!" said he; "talk of everything being useful! I am quite sure a stinging nettle is of no use in the world. See how it has stung my fingers! They are all over white blisters, and tingle terribly. I am quite sure grandpapa was wrong when he said that everything was useful."

"Perhaps not!" said the old gentleman, who at that moment peeped over the hedge; "but I will go round by the gate, and come to you."

In a few minutes the old gentleman was with them, examining the smarting fingers of his grandson.

"Well now, grandpapa, please to tell me of what use

nettles are—for I cannot think that they are of the least use whatever."

"The nettle has, no doubt, many uses," replied the old gentleman, "of which I am ignorant; but I will point out a few which may show you that God has not formed it in vain. And I may begin with the use the nettle has been of to you, Alfred."

"To me, grandpapa. I am quite sure it has been of no use to me."

"No!" said the old gentleman, smiling; "why, did it not save you from tumbling into the ditch?" Here Alfred looked rather foolish, while his grandpapa went on; "It is not a very long time ago, Alfred, since you were praising your nettle porridge. The porridge is made of the tender tops of young nettles; and I dare say you remember it very well."

"Oh yes!" said Mary. "It was old Esther Hodges who told my mother to give it to us; she said it would do us 'a power of good.'"

"I am glad you remember it; but let us look at the nettle a little nearer." Just then a bee alighted on one of the nettle flowers. "Do you think that bee, if he could speak, would say that the nettle was of no use? See, he is gathering honey from it, and, perhaps, finds it as useful as the blooming rose."

The old gentleman then set himself down on the bank; and, having his gloves on, he turned over some of the nettle leaves. "Look here," said he; "here is the insect called the ladybird, with its red back spotted with black: I dare say this ladybird finds the nettle of some use, or it would not take shelter under its leaves. Then, again, here is a spider who has woven his web from one leaf to another; no doubt the spider finds the nettle of some use too; so that the bee, the ladybird, and the spider are all against you."

Here Alfred and Mary looked at each other, as if now

quite satisfied that the nettle had not been made in vain. But their grandfather still went on:—"Nettles are often useful in keeping young people in the right path. When your sister begged you, Alfred, not to go near the ditch, you heeded her not; but when the nettle pointed out your error, you were convinced of it in a moment. The nettle. moreover, teaches a useful lesson. Look at Alfred's fingers; they are not stung where he grasped the nettle firmly, but only in the parts that touched it lightly. Many little trials of the world are of the same character: Give way to them, they annoy you; meet them bravely, they injure you not, for you overcome them. Another excellent lesson to be got from the nettle is, to mind your own business, and not to meddle with that of other people. Let the nettle alone, it never stings you; trespass upon it, you must take the consequences. I might say a good deal more; but if the nettle assists in forming a wholesome food—if it affords honey to the bee, shade and shelter to the ladybird and the spider,—if it keeps young people in the proper path, and furnishes us with lessons of useful instruction, you must allow that the stinging nettle has not been made in vain."

Old Humphrey.

THE DAISY AND THE LARK.

Gen-teel'	Scis'-sors	Con-ceive'
Fra'-grance	Thor'-ough	Anx'-ious
Pe'-o-nies	Rec'-og-nised	Quiv'-er-ing
Mu-si'-cian	Pris'-on-er	Or'-na-ments
I-mag'-ine	Dif'-fi-cult	La-ment'-ed

Out in the country, close by the road, stands a handsome house. Before it there is a garden with flowers, and a painted railing; and just outside the railing, among beautiful green grass, grew a little daisy. The sun shone upon it as warmly and kindly as upon the large, splendid flowers in the garden, and so it grew from hour to hour, till one morning it stood fully unfolded, wlth its small pure white petals in a ring round the little yellow sun in the middle. The daisy did not think at all that no one saw it there among the grass, and that it was a poor despised flower; no, it was very contented, turned its face to the warm sun, looked up to it, and listened to the lark singing high in the air.

Inside the railing stood a great many stiff, genteel flowers: the less fragrance they had the prouder they were of their fine dress. The peonies blew themselves up, in order to be bigger than the rose, but size is nothing! The tulips had the most beautiful colours, as they very well knew, and, therefore, they held themselves very straight up, that people might have a good sight of them. They never looked at the little daisy outside; but the daisy looked all the more at them, and thought within itself: "How rich and beautiful they are; certainly the lark will come down and pay them a visit; how glad I am that I am so near them, for then I shall see that fine musician too." Just at that moment—tee-wheet! down flew the lark, but not to the peonies and tulips; oh no, down into the grass beside the poor daisy, which was so astonished and so delighted that it did not know what to think. The bird danced round about it, and sang: "How soft the grass is; and see, what a lovely little flower, with a golden heart, and a silvery white dress!"

Nobody can imagine how happy the little daisy was. The lark kissed it with its bill, sang to it, and then flew up to the blue sky again. It was a full quarter of an hour before the daisy could compose itself, then it turned round to see what the garden flowers were doing;

surely, it thought, they must have been delighted to see a little flower so happy. But the tulips stood as stiff as before, and their lips were drawn together in a pout, and they were red in the face, for the fact was, they had been angry. The peonies hung their heavy heads in a very sulky manner, and it was as well they could not speak, otherwise the daisy would have got a thorough scolding. Just then a little girl came into the garden with a bright sharp pair of scissors, and went straight to the tulips all which she snipped off one after the other. "Oh, dear," sighed the daisy, "it is all over with them now." The girl went away with the tulips, but the daisy was glad that *its* head had not been snipped off, and very thankfully folded up its petals as the sun was setting, and fell asleep, and dreamed the whole night about the sun and the lark.

Next morning, as the flower was stretching out all its white petals, like so many little arms, to the air and light, it recognised the bird's voice, but the voice was very mournful now. The poor lark had, indeed, good reason for singing a sad song, for it had been taken prisoner, and put into a cage, which hung beside an open window of the house. The little daisy wished very much to help its friend the lark, but how was it to manage that? Yes, it was a difficult affair, the flower quite forgot how beautiful everything was all around it, and how warmly the sun shone, and could think of nothing but the captive bird.

Two little boys now came out of the garden, one of them with a knife in his hand, and they came directly towards the daisy, which could not conceive what they meant.

"Here we can cut out a beautiful piece of turf for the lark," said the boy with the knife, and immediately began to cut out a square turf, with the daisy exactly in the middle of it.

"Tear the flower off," said the other boy, and then the daisy began to tremble for fear. To be torn off was to lose its life, and it was so anxious to live, that it might come with the turf into the cage of the captive lark.

"No, let it stay!" said the first boy, "it makes the turf so pretty." The daisy was accordingly spared, and arrived with the turf in the cage of the prisoner.

But the poor bird lamented loudly over its lost freedom, and flapped with its wings against the wires of the cage; and the little daisy could not speak, could not say a word of comfort, willing as it was to do so. Thus passed the whole forenoon.

"There is no water here," said the imprisoned lark; "they have all gone out, and have forgotten to give me a drop of water to drink! My throat is dry and burning: ah! I must die." Then it bored its bill into the cool turf to refresh itself a little, and its eyes fell upon the daisy. The bird nodded to the flower, kissed it with its bill, and said: "Poor little flower, you will grow dry and wither away here too. They have given me only you, and your little spot of green grass, instead of the whole world that I had outside! Ah! you only remind me how much I have lost."

"Oh, if I could only comfort him!" thought the daisy. Evening came, but still no one brought the poor bird a drop of water. It stretched its pretty wings, and shook them in a quivering way that was painful to the daisy to see; its song was now a mournful chirp, its little head bent over the flower, and the bird's heart broke for want and longing. The flower could not now, as on the evening before, fold its petals together and sleep, it hung sickly and sad towards the ground.

The boys did not come till next morning, and when they saw the bird dead they cried, and shed many tears, and they dug it a neat little grave, which they decked with leaves of flowers. They had put the dead bird into a pretty red box, for they were resolved to give it a fine burial. Poor lark! while he lived and sang they forgot him, let him sit in his cage and suffer thirst, and now when he was dead, they gave him tears and ornaments.

The turf, with the daisy in the middle of it, was thrown out into the dusty road, and nobody thought of the one that had felt most pity for the poor bird, and had been most anxious to comfort it.

Hans Andersen.

SECTION II.

ENCOURAGEMENT TO TIMID CHILDREN.

Com-pan′-ions	Tor′-toise	Schol′-ar
School′-fel-lows	Dil′-i-gent	O-pin′-ion
En-cour′-age-ment	Slack′-en-ing	Ex-cus′-ing
Thought′-less-ness	Com-mand′-ments	At-ten′-tive

A word with you, my boys and girls, not you who are quick at your books and your play ; not you who are before your companions in learning ; not you who are always gay as larks, and light-hearted as lambs in a sunny field. But listen to me, you that are timid, and somewhat backward in your books. You that find it hard to learn, and cannot easily keep up with your school-fellows, listen patiently to Friend Barnaby.

There is no reason why you should be out of spirits : only be attentive, and do your best, and I will answer for your making progress in your studies.

It is said, that once on a time, a hare and a tortoise ran a race. The hare was by far the best runner, but, being vain and confident, she took a nap by the way. The tortoise got on very slowly, but being diligent, and never slackening her pace, she passed by the sleeping hare and won the race.

Now who can tell my little fearful friends, but that you, after all, by obedience, diligence, and plodding onwards, may win the race, and get more solid and useful knowledge, than those who run on so fast before you.

Some of the best trees are a long time in coming to perfection. Some of the best fruits ripen slowly, and many of the most learned men were at first, by no means clever scholars; therefore take courage and do your very best.

Mind, I am not excusing thoughtlessness and inattention, but only want of ability. If you are idle, careless, and disobedient, your are doing yourselves a great iujury; but if you are doing your best, again I say, Barnaby will answer for your success.

Your learning is not meant so much to make you clever, as it is to render you useful. He who has learned to fear God, to keep his commandments, and to love and serve those around him, is a better scholar in my opinion, than he who has learned Latin and Greek, but knows not how to make himself useful.

Friend Barnaby.

THE CHILDREN IN THE WOOD.

Now ponder well, you parents dear
  These words which I shall write;
A doleful story you shall hear,
  In time brought forth to light.
A gentleman of good account
  In Norfolk dwelt of late,
Whose wealth and riches did surmount
  Most men of his estate.

Sore sick he was, and like to die,
  No help his life could save;
His wife by him as sick did lie,
  And both possest one grave.

No love between these two was lost,
  Each was to other kind,
In love they lived, in love they died,
  And left two babes behind :

The one a fine and pretty boy,
  Not passing three years old ;
The other a girl more young than he,
  And made in beauty's mould.
The father left his little son,
  As plainly doth appear,
When he to perfect age should come,
  Three hundred pounds a year.

And to his little daughter Jane,
  Two hundred pounds in gold,
To be paid down on marriage-day,
  Which might not be controlled.
But if the children chanced to die,
  Ere they to age should come,
Their uncle should possess their wealth ;
  For so the will did run.

"Now brother," said the dying man,
  "Look to my children dear ;
Be good unto my boy and girl,
  No friends else have they here ;
To God and you I do commend
  My children night and day ;
A little while be sure we have
  Within this world to stay.

"You must be father and mother both
  And uncle, all in one ;
God knows what will become of them,
  When I am dead and gone."

With that bespake their mother dear,
  "O brother kind," quoth she,
"You are the man must bring my babes
  To wealth or misery:

"If you do keep them carefully,
  Then God will you reward;
If otherwise you seem to deal,
  God will your deeds regard."
With lips as cold as any stone,
  They kissed the children small:
"God bless you both my children dear!"
  With that the tears did fall.

These speeches then their brother spoke
  To this sick couple there;
"The keeping of your children dear,
  Sweet sister, do not fear;
God never prosper me nor mine,
  Nor aught else that I have,
If I do wrong your children dear,
  When you are laid in grave."

Their parents being dead and gone,
  The children home he takes,
And brings them both unto his house,
  Where much of them he makes.
He had not kept these pretty babes
  A twelvemonth and a day,
But, for their wealth, he did devise
  To make them both away.

He bargained with two ruffians rude,
  Which were of furious mood,
That they should take the children young,
  And slay them in a wood.

He told his wife and all he knew,
  He would the children send
To be brought up in fair London,
  With one that was his friend.

Away then went the pretty babes,
  Rejoicing at that tide,
Rejoicing with a merry mind
  They should on cock-horse ride.
They prate and prattle pleasantly,
  As they rode on the way,
To those that should their butchers be,
  And work their lives' decay;

So that the pretty speech they had,
  Made murderers' hearts relent:
And they that took the deed to do,
  Full sore they did repent.
Yet one of them, more hard of heart,
  Did vow to do his charge,
Because the wretch that hired him
  Had paid him very large.

The other would not agree thereto,
  So here they fell at strife;
With one another they did fight,
  About the children's life:
And he that was of mildest mood
  Did slay the other there,
Within an unfrequented wood,
  Where babes did quake for fear!

He took the children by the hand,
  When tears stood in their eye,
And bade them come and go with him,
  And look they did not cry:

And two long miles he led them thus,
While they for bread complain :
" Stay here," quoth he, " I'll bring ye bread,
When I do come again."

These pretty babes, with hand in hand,
Went wandering up and down ;
But never more they saw the man
Approachiug from the town ;
Their pretty lips with blackberries,
Were all besmeared and dyed,
And when they saw the darksome night,
They sat them down and cried.

Thus wandered these two pretty babes,
Till death did end their grief,
In one another's arms they died,
As babes wanting relief :
No burial these pretty babes
Of any man receives,
Till robin red-breast painfully
Did cover them with leaves.

And now the heavy wrath of God
Upon their uncle fell ;
Yea, fearful fiends did haunt his house
His conscience felt a hell :
His barns were fired, his goods consumed,
His lands were barren made ;
His cattle died within the field,
And nothing with him stayed.

And in the voyage of Portugal
Two of his sons did die ;
And, to conclude, himself was brought
Unto much misery :

He pawned and mortgaged all his land
  Ere seven years came about;
And now at length this wicked act
  Did by this means come out:

The fellow, that did take in hand
  These children for to kill,
Was for a robbery judged to die,
  As was God's blessed will:
Who did confess the very truth,
  The which is here exprest;
Their uncle died while he for debt
  Did long in prison rest.

All you that be executors,
  And overseers eke,
Of children that be fatherless,
  And infants mild and meek;
Take you example by this thing,
  And yield to each his right,
Lest God with such like misery
  Your wicked minds requite.

Old Ballad.

THE DISHONEST BUTLER.

A-gree'-ment	Dif'-fer-ent	But'-ler
Des-ti-na'-tion	Sov'-e-reign	Dis-hon'-est
As-sist'-ance	Ear'-nest-ness	Char'-ac-ter
Ap-par'-ent	Cov'-et-ous-ness	Sit-u-a'-tion

Some time ago, a noble Duke, in one of his walks, bought a cow, and left orders to have it sent to his house the following morning. According to the agreement the cow was sent, and the Duke who happened to be walking in the grounds, saw a little fellow trying in vain to drive the animal to its destination. The boy not knowing his Grace, sung out to him, "Come here, and lend us a hand wi' this beast."

The Duke saw the mistake, and determined on having a joke with the little fellow. Pretending therefore not to understand him, he walked on slowly, the boy still craving his assistance. At last the boy cried out in a tone of apparent distress: "Come here man, and help us; and as sure as I'm a man I'll give you half I get!" This last appeal had the desired effect.

The Duke went and lent a helping hand. "And now," said he, as they trudged along, "how much do you think you'll get for this job?" "Oh, I dont know," said the boy; "but I'm sure o' something, for the folk up at the house are good to everybody." As they approached the house, the Duke darted from the boy and entered by a different way. He called a servant, and put a sovereign into his hand, saying: "Give that to the boy who has brought the cow."

He returned to the walk, and was soon rejoined by the boy. "Well, how much did you get?" said the former. "A shilling, and there's the half o' it to ye." "But you *surely got* more than a shilling!" "No," said the boy, with the utmost earnestness, "that's all I got—d'ye not think it's plenty!" "I do not; there must be some mistake, and, if you return I fancy I can get you more." The boy consented; so back they went.

The Duke rang the bell, and ordered all the servants to be assembled. "Now," said his Grace to the boy, "point me out the person that gave you the shilling." "It was that man there," pointing to the butler. The guilty man confessed his crime, and attempted an excuse, but his Grace stopped him; ordered him to give the boy the sovereign, and to quit his service instantly. "You have lost," said he, "your money, your situation, and your character, by your covetousness; learn, henceforth, to be honest." *Anon.*

BOOKS.

Mil′-lions	Pyr′-a-mids	Eu′-rope
Im-por′-tant	An′-cient	Na′-tions
Ear′-ly	E-gyp′-tians	An′-ces-tors
Coun′-tries	Stat′-ues	Con′-quered
Fa′-mous	Bab-y-lo′-ni-ans	Care′-ful-ly

There are so many wise and good things written in books, that you ought to try to read early and carefully. There are many thousands of books, and all that is written in them is either about the world which God has made, or about the thoughts which he has enabled men to have in their minds. Some books describe the earth itself, with its rocks, and ground, and water ; or the air and clouds ; or the stars, and moon, and sun, which shine so beautifully in the sky. Some tell you about the things that grow upon the ground—the many millions of plants, from little mosses and threads of grass, up to the great trees and forests. Some also contain accounts of living things ; flies, worms, fishes, birds, and four-legged beasts. And some, which are the most, are about men, and their thoughts and doings.

These books about men are the most important to us ; for men are the most wonderful creatures of God in this world ; being the only ones able to know and love him, and to try of their own accord to do his will. Besides we ourselves are human beings, and may learn from such books what we ought to think, and to do, and try to be. Some of them describe what sort of people have lived in old times, and in other countries. By reading them we know what is the difference between ourselves in England now, and the famous nations which lived in former days. Such were the Egyptians, who built the Pyramids—the greatest heaps of stone on the face of the earth; and the Babylonians, who had a city with huge walls, built of bricks, having writing on them that no one in our time has been able to make out fully. There were also the Jews, who were the only ancient people that knew God; and the Greeks, who knew best how to make fine statues and buildings, and to write books. By books, also, we may learn what sort of people the old Romans were, whose chief city was Rome, and how brave and skilful they were in war, and how well they could govern the nations which they had conquered. It is from books, too, that you must learn what kind of men were our ancestors in the northern part of Europe, before they came to live here in England; and you will see in the same way how the gospel was sent among them by God, to make them wiser and more peaceful, and more noble in their minds.

Besides learning all these things, you may also learn from books what are the best and wisest thoughts, and the most beautiful words; and how men are able to lead right lives, and to do a great deal to better the world. If you try to be better for all you read, as well as wiser, you will find books a great help towards goodness as well as knowledge,—and above all other books, the Bible, which tells us of the will of God, and of the love of Jesus Christ.

John Sterling.

THE DAISY,

The daisy is the meekest flower
That grows in wood or field:
To wind and rain, and footstep rude,
Its slender stem will yield.

And when they 're passed away again,
As cheerfully it springs,
As if a playful butterfly
Had bent it with his wings.

The daisy is a hardy plant,
  And in the winter time,
We find it by the sheltered nooks,
  Unhurt by snow and rime.

In spring it dots the green with white,
  It blossoms all the year,
And so it is a fav'rite flower,
  To little children dear.

Before the stars are in the sky,
  The daisy goes to rest,
And folds its little shining leaves,
  Upon its golden breast.

And so it sleeps in dewy night,
  Until the morning breaks,
Then with the songs of early birds,
  So joyously awakes.

And children, when they go to bed,
  Should fold their hands in prayer,
And place themselves, and all they love,
  In God's almighty care.

Then they may sleep secure and still,
  Through hours of darksome night,
And with the pretty daisy wake,
  In cheerful morning light.

Little Poems for Little People.

THE CHILD'S WISH IN JUNE.

Mother, mother, the winds are at play,
Prithee let me be idle to day ;
Look, dear mother, the flowers all lie
Languidly under the bright blue sky;

See how slowly the streamlet glides ;
Look how the violet roguishly hides ;
Even the butterfly rests on the rose,
And scarcely sips the sweets as he goes.

Poor Tray is asleep in the noon-day sun,
And the flies go about him one by one;
And Pussy sits near, with a sleepy grace,
Without ever thinking of washing her face.
There flies a bird to a neighbouring tree,
But very lazily flieth he ;
And he sits and twitters a gentle note,
That scarcely ruffles his little throat.

You bid me be busy; but mother, hear
How the hum-drum grasshopper soundeth near;
And the soft west wind is so light in his play,
It scarcely moves a leaf on the spray.
I wish, oh, I wish I was yonder cloud
That sails about in its misty shroud ;
Books and work, I no more should see,
And I'd come and float, dear mother, o'er thee.

School-room Lyrics.

HEROISM OF A MINER.

Corn'-ish	Re-quired'	Ex-plo'-sion
Af-fair'	Hor'-ri-ble	Bruis'-ing
Sig'-nal	Ve'-he-ment-ly	De-scend'-ing
Hoist'-ed	Wind'-lass	Ea'-ger-ly
Suc-ceed'-ed	Re-signs'	Mir'-a-cle

In a certain Cornish mine, two miners, deep down in the shaft, were engaged in putting in a shot for blasting. They had completed their affair, and were about to give the signal for being hoisted up. One at a time was all the assistant at the top could manage, and the

was to kindle the match, and then mount with
l.

it chanced, while they were still below, that
hem thought the match too long. He accord-
ied to break it shorter. Taking a couple of
a flat and a sharp, he succeeded in cutting it
iired length ; but horrible to relate, he kindled
same time, while both were still below! Both
vehemently to the man at the windlass ; both
at the basket. The windlass man could not
with both in it.

was a moment for poor miner Jack and miner
Instant, horrible death hangs over them. Will
sly resigns himself. "Go aloft, Jack ; sit
away! in one minute I shall be in heaven!"
bounds aloft, the explosion instantly follows,
; his face as he looks over ; but he is safe above

what of poor Will? Descending eagerly, they
1, as if by miracle, buried under rocks which had
;hemselves over him. He is little injured. He
rought up safe. Well done brave Will!

Thomas Carlyle.

USTLING WAY AND THE QUIET WAY.

tle	Mor′-ti-fied	Thim′-ble
′-dient	Di-rec′-tion	Ea′-si-ly
-ent	Per-ceiv′-ing	Im-prop′-er
r-rupt′-ed	Sor′-row-ful	Pa-rade′
lour	In′-do-lent	Op-por-tu′-ni-ties
umes	Pos′-si-ble	Pref′-er-ence
-ra′-tion	Hearth′-rug	Through-out′
a′-sion-ing	Shov′-el	Con-tin′-u-ing
-ing	Chim′-ney-piece	Re-proof′

e are some children who do very little good,
hen they wish to be of use to others, because

they make so much bustle about everything they undertake.

Jane Riddell is one of these bustling characters. She is always ready and willing to help her mother whom she loves very much, and to whom she is always obedient ; but she makes so much noise and talk about any little thing she has to do, that one would rather do it ten times over than be present while she is doing it.

"Mother," said Jane, one morning when she sat reading, "Mother, mother"! calling several times before her mother had time to look up. Jane ought not to have interrupted her mother while she was reading,—she had nothing really important to say. "Mother, mother, I want to know whether I may go and put the back parlour to rights."

"Yes, yes, you may," said her mother, going on with her reading.

"Well—mother, mother!"

"What now, Jane ?"

"May I take down all the books from the shelves, and put them up better ? I know I can put them up right again. May I, mother ? "

"Yes, you may ; but do not talk to me now because I am engaged. "

Jane went to work, making a great noise in taking down and in putting up the books. Instead of clearing one shelf at a time, and fitting it before she cleared the next, she took down all the books at once ; and as she stood on a chair to replace them she must needs jump down for each parcel as she set them up again.

"O Jane," her mother would now and then exclaim, as the volumes came tumbling upon the floor, "do be a little more careful, and try to make less noise."

But for Jane to have carried on any operation without making a great fuss, or occasioning interruption to other persons, would have been quite out of the question.

"There mother, just come and see how much better that looks," she said each time she had filled a shelf.

Because her mother did not attend at once, she went on calling "Mother, mother," until at last, becoming quite tired of being interrupted, her mother bade her leave the room as it was, and sit down to her sewing. Jane felt mortified and grieved at the reproof thus conveyed, and could scarcely repress her tears as she prepared to obey the direction.

"Why, what is the matter, Jane?" said her mother, laying down her book and perceiving Jane's sorrowful looks. This question brought the tears at once into Jane's eyes.

"Why, mother," she answered, "I was putting the book-shelves to rights as well as I could, when you spoke to me, and—and, I was going—"

"Well, you did them very well, and I should have been glad had you finished them; but you made so much bustle about it, and talked so much, that I could not go on with my reading. I have never spoken to you particularly about this fault, but it is one that you can easily overcome. You are a very lively, active, little girl; I should be sorry were you indolent and dull; but when you have anything to do, I wish you to do it with as little noise and bustle as possible.

"Now, I will show you the difference between the bustling and the quiet way of doing things. Let me see, —what shall I do? Oh! there is the hearth-rug which is out of order." One edge of the rug was turned under, and Jane's mother walked to the fire-place, stooped down to the rug, and with one or two strokes of her hand, spread it even, and smoothed out the fringe. "There, that is the quiet way of doing the thing; now I will show you the bustling way." Her mother then hurried to the fire-place, pulled away the chairs that stood near, rattled the shovel and tongs; then turned over the rug in such a manner as to cause a great puff of smoke and dust from the fire; and then, in the same parading style, spread the rug down again. "That is the bustling way of doing it," said her mother, sweeping up the hearth, and brushing off the ashes that had settled upon the chimney-piece.

"Now I will show you how it is for persons to talk and disturb others while they are engaged. Let us suppose that you have lost your thimble, and that I am going to look after it for you." She then pretended to be looking for the lost thimble; "Why, Jane," said she, hastily turning over the things on the table, "where *do* you suppose your thimble can be? Surely Susan must have mislaid it when she swept the parlour. I wish she were not such a careless girl." She then went to another part of the room, and looked under the sofa, continuing all the while to talk: "Why, Jane, perhaps you left your thimble up stairs; did you not? Jane—Jane—Jane, did you not leave your thimble up stairs? shall I go up and see?"

Jane stood laughing to see her mother acting in this strange way.

"You think it odd for me to act in such a manner," said her mother, "but it is quite as improper in a little girl like you. Now," she continued, "I wish you to learn the quiet way of doing things, and then you will be much more useful to me than you are at present; for very often when there is something that you could do, I say, 'No, I will do it myself, for Jane will have so much to say, and will make such a parade about it, that she will cause me more trouble than she will save.' But I wish you to begin now to learn the quiet way of going about everything, and then you will be a very great help to me."

Jane had many opportunities throughout the day of practising her new lesson, and she felt amply repaid by ıer mother's smile, and approving looks, and resolved ·ver afterwards to try the quiet way in preference to the ›ustling way.

Abbott.

MOTHER WHAT IS DEATH?

"Mother, how still the baby lies!
I cannot hear his breath;
I cannot see his laughing eyes—
They tell me this is death.

My little work I thought to bring,
And sat down by his bed;
And pleasantly I tried to sing—
They hushed me—he is dead.

They say that he again will rise,
More beautiful than now;
That God will bless him in the skies—
Oh, mother tell me how!"

"Daughter, do you remember, dear,
The cold, dark thing you brought,
And laid upon the casement here,—
A withered worm you thought?

I told you that Almighty power
Could break that withered shell,
And show you in a future hour,
Something would please you well.

Look at the chrysalis, my love,
An empty shell it lies;
Now raise your wond'ring glance above,
To where yon insect flies!"

"Oh, yes, mamma! how very gay
  Its wings of starry gold!
And, see! it lightly flies away
  Beyond my gentle hold.

Oh! mother, now I know full well,
  If God that worm can change,
And draw it from this broken cell,
  On golden wings to range.

How beautiful will brother be,
  When God shall give him wings,
Above this dying world to flee,
  And live with heavenly things!"

Jane Gilman.

BE KIND.

Be kind to thy father: for when thou wert young,
  Who loved thee as fondly as he?
He caught the first accents that fell from thy tongue,
  And joined in thine innocent glee:
Be kind to thy father, for now he is old,
  His locks intermingled with grey;
His footsteps are feeble, once fearless and bold;
  Thy father is passing away.

Be kind to thy mother: for lo! on her brow
  May traces of sorrow be seen;
O well mayst thou cherish and comfort her now,
  For loving and kind hath she been.
Remember thy mother: for thee will she pray,
  As long as God giveth thee breath;
With accents of kindness, then, cheer her lone way,
  E'en to the dark valley of death.

Be kind to thy brother: his heart will have dearth,
If the smile of thy love be withdrawn;
The flowers of feeling will fade at their birth,
If the dew of affection be gone.
Be kind to thy brother: wherever you are,
The love of a brother shall be
An ornament, purer and richer by far
Than pearls from the depths of the sea.

Be kind to thy sister: not many may know
The depth of true sisterly love;
The wealth of the ocean has fathoms below
The surface that sparkles above.
Thy kindness shall bring to thee many sweet hours,
And blessings thy pathway to crown;
Affection shall weave thee a garland of flowers,
More precious than wealth or renown.

Anon.

THE DIFFERENCE BETWEEN A LIAR AND A BOY OF TRUTH.

Sor′-ry	Where′-a-bouts	Ex-cuse′
Mon′-day	Cow′-ard-ly	Switch
Fright′-ened	De-ter′-mined	Neigh′-bour-hood
Re-mem′-ber	Per-suade′	Col′-lar
Ad-vise′	Col′-oured	Sig′-ni-fy
Be-lieve′	Hes′-i-ta-ted	Be-tween′

"Come," said Robert to Frank, "there is Trusty lying beside the fire, asleep; let us go and waken him, and he will play with us."—"O yes, do let us," said Frank. So they both ran together, towards the hearth, to waken the dog.

Now there was a basin of milk standing upon the

hearth, and the little boys did not see whereabouts it stood. As they were both playing with the dog, they kicked it with their feet, and threw it down; and the basin broke, and all the milk ran out: and, when the little boys saw what they had done, they were very sorry and frightened. Robert spoke first. "So we shall have no milk for supper to-night," said he and sighed. "No milk for supper! why not," said Frank, "is there no milk in the house?" "Yes; but we shall have none of it: for do not you remember last Monday, when we threw down the milk, mother said we were very careless, and that the next time we did so we should have no milk for supper?" "Well, then," said Frank, "we must do without it, that's all; we will take more care another time: come let's run and tell mother. You know she bid us always tell her directly when we broke any thing." "I will come just now," said Robert; "dont be in such a hurry, Frank, can't you stay a minute?" So Frank staid; and then he said, "Come now, Robert." But Robert answered, "Stay a little longer, for I dare not go yet. I am afraid."

Little boys, I advise you never be afraid to tell the truth; never say "stay a minute," and "stay a little longer," but run directly and tell what you have done that is wrong. The longer you stay, the more afraid you will grow; till, at last, perhaps, you will not dare to tell the truth at all. Hear what happened to Robert. The longer he staid the more unwilling he was to go to tell his mother that he had thrown the milk down; and at last Frank went without him in search of his mother.

Now whilst Frank was gone, Robert was left in the room by himself; and all the while he was alone he was thinking of some excuses to make to his mother. He said to himself, "If Frank and I both were to say that we did not throw down the basin, she would believe us, and we should have milk for supper! I am very sorry Frank would go to tell her about it." Just as he said this to himself, he heard his mother coming down stairs. "O ho!" said he to himself, and so Frank has not met her and cannot have told her, so I may say what I please." Then this cowardly boy determined to tell his mother a lie.

She came into the room; but when she saw the broken basin and the milk spilled, she stopped short, and cried, "So, so, what a piece of work is here—who did this, Robert?" "I don't know, ma'am," said Robert, in a very low voice. "You don't know, Robert!—tell me the truth—I shall not be angry with you—I would rather have you break all the basins I have, than to tell one lie;—I ask you Robert, did you break the basin?" "No, ma'am, I did not," said Robert, and he coloured as red as fire. "Then where's Frank?—did he do it?" "No, mother, he did not," said Robert; for he was in hopes that when Frank came in, he should persuade him to say that he did not do it. "How do you know," said his mother, "that Frank did not do it?" "Because—because—because, ma'am," said Robert, hesitating as liars do for an excuse, "because I was in the room all the time, and I did not see him do it." "Then how was the basin thrown down? If you have been in the room all the time you can tell." Then Robert, going on from one lie to another, answered, "I suppose the dog must have done it." "Did you see him do it?" said his mother. "Yes," said this wicked boy. "Trusty, Trusty," said his mother, turning round, "Fie! fie! Trusty, get me a switch out of the garden, Robert, Trusty must be beat for this."—Robert ran for the switch, and in the garden he met his brother; he stopped him, and told him in a great hurry all that he had said to his mother, and begged of him not to tell the truth, but to say the same that he had done. "No, I will not tell a lie," said Frank, "what! and is Trusty to be beat! He did not throw down the milk, and he shan't be beat for it. Let me go to my mother." They both ran towards the house. Robert got first home, and he locked the house-door, that Frank might not come in. He gave the switch to his mother. Poor Trusty, he looked up as the switch was lifted over his head; but HE could not speak to tell the truth. Just as the blow was falling upon him, Frank's voice was heard at the window. "Stop, stop! dear mother, stop!" cried he, as loud as ever he could call; "Trusty did not do it—I and Robert did it; but do not beat Robert." "Let us in, let us in," cried another voice, which Robert knew to be his father's voice; for his father always whipped him when he told a lie. His mother went to the door and unlocked it. "What's all this?" cried his father as he came in: so his mother told him all that had happened.—"Where is the switch with which you were going to beat Trusty?" said their father. Then Robert, who saw by his father's looks that he was going to beat him, fell upon his knees, and cried for mercy, saying, "Forgive me this time and I will never tell a lie again." But his father caught hold of him by the arm; "I will whip you now," said he, "and then I hope you will not." So Robert was whipped till he cried so loud with the pain that the whole neighbourhood could hear him. "There," said his father, when he had done, "now, go without supper: you are to have no milk to-night, and you have been whipped. See how liars are served." Then turning to Frank, "Come here and shake hands with me, Frank: you will have no milk for supper, but that does not signify; you have told the truth, and have not been whipped, and every body is pleased with you. And now I'll tell you what I will do for you,—I will give you the little dog Trusty to be your own dog; you have saved him a beating, and I'll answer for it you'll be a good master to him. To-morrow I'll go to the brazier's and get a new collar made for him: from this day forward he shall be called after you, FRANK! And, wife, whenever any of the neighbours' children ask you why the dog TRUSTY is to be called FRANK, tell them this story of our two boys; let them know the difference between a liar and a boy of truth!"

Miss Edgeworth.

"LOVE COVERETH ALL SINS."

Ac-cused′	Dis-grace′	Hon′-our
Cit′-rons	Sus-pect′-ed	Glo′-ri-ous
Pro-test′-ed	Guilt′-y	Fur′-ther
In′-no-cent	Con-sid-e-ra′-tion	Mis′-chief
Pun′-ish-ment	False′-hood	De-lib′-e-rate

It is related of Napoleon I., that when he was a child of seven years of age, he was one day accused by one of his sisters of having eaten a basket-full of grapes, figs, and citrons, which had come from the garden of his uncle. Napoleon denied that he had eaten them; but it was believed that he had, and he was whipped. He was told that if he would beg pardon he should be forgiven. He, however, protested that he was innocent, but he was not believed. As a further punishment he was kept three whole days upon bread and cheese. However, he did not cry, though he was dull, but not sulky. At length, on the fourth day of his punishment, a little friend of another of his sisters, Marianne Bonaparte, returned from the country, and on hearing of Napoleon's disgrace, she confessed that she and Marianne had eaten the fruit. It was now Marianne's turn to be punished. When Napoleon was asked why he had not accused his sister, he replied, that though he suspected that she was guilty, yet out of consideration to her little friend who had no share in the falsehood, he had said nothing. Now this was covering the sin of his little friend. He scorned to be a tell-tale, even at the expense of suffering himself. Napoleon did this, perhaps, from what is called a high sense of honour ; and there was something noble in his conduct. When he grew to be a man he did many things falsely called glorious ; but he never looked so glorious as when on this occasion he scorned to tell a lie, and charge himself with taking the fruit to save further punishment, and he would not tell of others to get them punished.

If we can prevent mischief we should do so ; but when it is done let us not be the first to tell of it, that we may injure others. Let us warn them against doing it again ; and if it is designed and deliberate mischief let us avoid both them and their doings.

Cobbin.

THE SUNSHINE.

I love the sunshine everywhere—
In wood, and field, and glen,
I love it in the busy haunts
Of town-imprisoned men.

I love it, when it streameth in
The humble cottage door,
And casts the chequered casement shade
Upon the red-brick floor.

I love it, where the children lie
Deep in the clovery grass,
To watch among the twining roots,
The gold-green beetle pass.

I love it, on the breezy sea,
To glance on sail and oar,

While the great waves, like molten glass,
Come leaping to the shore.

I love it, on the mountain-tops,
Where lies the thawless snow;
And half a kingdom, bathed in light,
Lies stretching out below.

Oh! yes, I love the sunshine!
Like kindness, or like mirth,
Upon a human countenance,
Is sunshine on the earth.

Upon the earth—upon the sea—
And through the crystal air—
Or piled-up clouds—the gracious sun
Is glorious everywhere.

Mary Howitt.

A NOBLEMAN AND HIS NOBLE SERVANT.

Daugh'-ter	Car'-riage	De-struc'-tion
En-treat'-ed	Dis-tinct'-ly	Ag-o-nis'-ing
Pis'-tols	Com'-rades	Ar-rest'
No'-ble-man	Af-fright'	De-vot'-ed
Pur-suit'	Mus'-ket	E-rect'-ed

A Russian nobleman was travelling in the early part of the winter over a bleak plain. His carriage rolled up to an inn, and he demanded a relay of horses to go on. The inn-keeper entreated him not to proceed, for there was danger abroad; the wolves were out. He thought the object of the man was to keep him as a guest for the night; and saying it was too early in the season for wolves, ordered the horses to be put to. In spite of the continued warnings of the landlord, the carriage drove away with the nobleman, his wife, and their only daughter.

On the box of the carriage was a serf, who had been born on the nobleman's estate, and who loved his master as he loved his life. They rolled on over the hardened snow, and there seemed no signs of danger. The moon began to shed her light, so that the road appeared like polished silver. At length the little girl said to her father, "What is that strange dull sound that I just heard?" Her father replied, "Nothing but the wind sighing through the trees of the forest we have just passed." The child shut her eyes and was quieted for the time; but in a few minutes, with a face pale with affright, she turned to her father, and said, "Surely that was not the wind; I heard it again, did you not hear it too? Listen!" The nobleman listened, and far, far away in the distance behind him, but distinct enough in the clear, frosty air, he heard a sound which he knew the meaning of, though they did not.

He put down the glass, and, speaking to the serf, said, "I think they are after us; we must make haste: tell the post-boy to drive faster, and get your musket and pistols ready; I will do the same; we may yet escape."

The man drove faster; but the mournful howling, which the child had first heard, began to come nearer and nearer, and it was perfectly clear to the nobleman that a pack of wolves had got scent and were in pursuit of them. Meanwhile he tried to calm the anxious fears of his wife and child. At last the baying of the pack was distinctly heard, and he said to his servant, "When they come up with us, single you out the leader and fire; I will single out the next, and, as soon as one falls, the rest will stop to devour him: *that* will be some delay at least."

By this time they could see the pack fast approaching with their long measured tread, a large dog-wolf leading. They singled out two, and they fell; the pack immediately turned upon their fallen comrades and soon tore them to pieces. The taste of blood only made the others advance with more fury, and they were again soon baying at the carriage. Again the nobleman and his servant fired, and two more fell, which were instantly devoured as before; but the next post-house was still far distant.

The nobleman then cried to the post-boy, "You must let one of the horses loose from the carriage, in order that, when the wolves come up to him, their destruction of the horse may gain us a little time." This was done, and the horse was left on the road: in a few minutes they heard the loud agonising shriek of the poor animal as the wolves tore him down. Again they urged on the carriage, but again their enemies were in full pursuit. A second horse was sent adrift, and shared the same fate as his fellow.

At length the servant said to his master, "I have served you since I was a child, and I love you as I love my own life; it is perfectly clear to me that we cannot all reach the post-house alive; I am quite prepared, and I ask you to let me die for you." "No," said the master, "we will live together, or die together; it must not be so." But the entreaties of the man at length prevailed, "I shall leave my wife and children to you; you will be a father to them; you have been a father to me; when the wolves next reach us, I will jump down and do the best I can to arrest their progress."

The carriage rolls on as fast as the two remaining horses can drag it; the wolves are close on their track, and almost dash against the doors of the carriage. Presently is heard the discharge of the servant's pistols as he leaps from his seat. Soon the door of the post-house is reached, and the family is safe.

They went to the spot the following morning where the wolves had pulled the devoted servant to pieces. There now stands a large wooden cross, erected by the nobleman, with this text upon it,—"Greater love hath no man than this, that one lay down his life for his friend."

Champneys.

THE SEASONS.

Ap-proach′-es	Lan′-guid	Par′-tridge
Mar′-ble	Riv′-u-lets	Pheas′-ant
Trans-pa′-rent	Ac′-id	I′-ci-cles
Sul′-try	Twi′-light	Pier′-cing
Re-fresh′-ment	Un-a-wares′	Flut′-ter
Crys′-tal	Au′-burn	Plen′-ti-ful-ly

Who is this beautiful Virgin that approaches, clothed in a robe of light green? She has a garland of flowers on her head, and flowers spring up wherever she sets her foot. The snow which covered the fields, and the ice, which was in the rivers, melt away when she breathes upon them. The young lambs frisk about her, and the birds warble in their little throats to welcome her coming; and when they see her, they begin to choose their mates, and to build their nests. Youths and maidens, have ye seen this beautiful Virgin? If ye have, tell me who she is, and what is her name.

Who is this that cometh from the south, thinly clad in a light transparent garment? Her breath is hot and sultry; she seeks the refreshment of the cool shade; she seeks the clear streams, the crystal brooks to bathe her languid limbs. The brooks and rivulets fly from her, and are dried up at her approach. She cools her parched lips with berries, and the grateful acid of all fruits; the seedy melon, the sharp apple, and the red pulp of the juicy cherry, which are poured out plentifully around her. The tanned haymakers welcome her coming, and the sheep-shearer, who clips the fleeces off his flock with the sounding shears. When she cometh, let me lie under the thick shade of a spreading beech-tree —let me walk with her in the early morning, when the dew is yet upon the grass—let me wander with her in the soft twilight, when the shepherd shuts his fold and the star of evening appears. Who is she that cometh from the south? Youths and maidens, tell me, if you know, who is she, and what is her name?

Who is he that cometh with sober pace, stealing upon us unawares? His garments are red with the blood of the grape, and his temples are bound with a sheaf of ripe wheat. His hair is thin and begins to fall, and the auburn is mixed with mournful grey. He shakes the brown nuts from the tree. He winds the horn, and calls the hunters to their sport. The gun sounds—the trembling partridge and the beautiful pheasant flutter bleeding in the air, and fall dead at the sportsman's feet. Who is he that is crowned with the wheat-sheaf? Youths and maidens, tell me if ye know, who is he, and what is his name?

Who is he that cometh from the north, clothed in furs and warm wool? He wraps his cloak close about him. His head is bald, his beard is made of sharp icicles. He loves the blazing fire high piled upon the hearth, and the wine sparkling in the glass. His breath is piercing and cold, and no little flower dares to peep above the surface of the ground when he is by. Whatever he touches turns to ice. If he were to stroke you with his cold hand, you would be quite stiff and dead like a piece of marble. Youths and maidens, do you see him? He is coming fast upon us, and soon he will be here. Tell me, if you know, who he is, and what is his name?

Evenings at Home.

THE VOICE OF SPRING.

I am coming! I am coming!—
Hark! the little bee is humming;
See, the lark is soaring high
In the blue and sunny sky;
And the gnats are on the wing,
Wheeling round in airy ring.

See the yellow catkins cover
All the slender willows over;
And on banks of mossy green
Star-like primroses are seen;
And, their clustering leaves below
White and purple violets blow.

Hark! the new-born lambs are bleating,
And the cawing rooks are meeting
In the elms—a noisy crowd!
All the birds are singing loud;
And the first white butterfly
In the sunshine dances by.

Look around thee—look around!
Flowers in all the fields abound;
Every running stream is bright;
All the orchard trees are white,
And each small and waving shoot
Promises sweet flowers and fruit.

Turn thine eyes to earth and heaven!
God for thee the spring has given,
Taught the birds their melodies,
Clothed the earth, and cleared the skies,
For thy pleasure or thy food:—
Pour thy soul in gratitude!

Mary Howitt.

THE TYROLESE EVENING HYMN.

Come, come, come!
Come to the sunset-tree:
The day is past and gone,
The woodman's axe lies free,
And the reaper's work is done.
The twilight star to heaven,
And the summer dew to flowers;
And rest to us is given,
By the cool, soft, evening hours.
Come, come, come!

Sweet is the hour of rest,
Pleasant the wind's low sigh;
And the gleaming of the west,
And the turf whereon we lie;
When the burden and the heat
Of labour's task are o'er;
And kindly voices greet
The tired one at the door.
Come, come, come!

Yes! tuneful is the sound
That dwells in whispering boughs;
Welcome the freshness round,
And the gale that fans our brows.
But rest more sweet and still
Than ever night-fall gave,
Our yearning hearts shall fill,
In the world beyond the grave.
Come, come, come!

There shall no tempests blow,
No scorching noon-tide heat;
There shall be no more snow,
No weary, wandering feet.

So we lift our trusting eyes,
From the hills our father's trod,
To the quiet of the skies,
To the Sabbath of our God!
Come, come, come!

Mrs. Hemans.

BRAVE JEM.—Part I.

Straw'-ber-ry	Med'-i-cines	Mon'-day
Nose'-gay	Re-source'	Fort'-night
Chief'-ly	In-dus'-tri-ous	Guin'-eas
O-blig'-ing	Em'-bers	Val'-ley
Ne-glect'-ed	Op'-po-site	Sig'-ni-fies

In the pleasant valley of Ashton there lived an elderly woman of the name of Preston. She had a small neat cottage, and there was not a weed to be seen in her garden. It was upon her garden that she chiefly depended for support: it consisted of strawberry-beds, and one small border for flowers. The pinks and roses she tied up in nice nosegays, and sent either to Clifton or Bristol to be sold. As to her strawberries, she did not send them to market, because it was the custom for numbers of people to come from Clifton, in the summer time, to eat strawberries and cream at the gardens in Ashton.

Now the widow Preston was so obliging, active, and good-tempered, that every one who came to see her was pleased. She lived happily in this manner for several years; but, alas! one autumn she fell sick, and, during her illness, everything went wrong: her garden was neglected, her cow died, and all the money which she had saved was spent in paying for medicines. Winter passed away, while she continued so weak that she could earn but little by her work; and when summer came, her rent was called for, and this was not ready in her little purse as usual. She begged a few months' delay, and they were granted; but at the end of that time there was no resource but to sell her horse Lightfoot.

Now, Lightfoot, though perhaps he had seen his best days was a very great pet; in his youth he had always carried the dame to market behind her husband; and it was now her little son Jem's turn to ride him. It was Jem's business to feed Lightfoot, and to take care of him; a charge which he never neglected, for, besides being very good-natured, he was a very industrious boy.

"It will go near to break my Jem's heart," said dame Preston to herself, as she sat one evening beside the fire, stirring the embers, and considering how she had best open the matter to her son, who stood opposite to her, eating a dry crust of bread very heartily for supper.

"Jem," said the old woman, "what, art hungry?"

"That I am, brave and hungry!"

"Aye! no wonder, you've been brave hard at work —Eh?"

"Brave hard! I wish it was not so dark, mother, that you might just step out and see the great bed I've dug; I know you'd say it was no bad day's work—and, oh mother! I've good news; farmer Truck will give us the giant-strawberries, and I'm to go for them to-morrow morning, and I'll be back before breakfast."

"Bless the boy! how he talks! Four miles there and four back again, before breakfast."

"Aye upon Lightfoot, you know mother, very easily, —mayn't I?"

"Aye, aye, child!"

"Why do you sigh, mother?"

"Finish thy supper, child."

"I've done!" cried Jem, swallowing the last mouthful hastily, as if he thought he had been too long at supper. "And now for the great needle, I must see and mend Lightfoot's bridle before I go to bed." To work he set, by the light of the fire; and the dame having once more stirred it, began again with "Jem, dear, does he go lame at all now?" "What Lightfoot! Oh no, not he!—never was so well of his lameness in all his life, he's grown quite young again, I think; and then he's so fat he can hardly wag." "Bless him—that's right—we must see, Jem, and keep him fat."

"For what, mother?"

"For Monday fortnight at the fair.' He's to be sold!"

"Lightfoot!" cried Jem, as the bridle dropped from his hand; "and will mother sell Lightfoot?"

"*Will!* no: but *must*, Jem."

"Must; who says you *must?* why *must* you, mother?"

"I must, I say, child. Why, must I not pay my debts honestly—and must I not pay my rent; and was it not called for long and long ago; and have not I had time: and did I not promise to pay it for certain Monday fortnight, and am I not two guineas short—and where am I to get two guineas? So what signifies talking, child?" said the widow, leaning her head upon her arm, "Lightfoot must go."

Jem was silent for a few minutes. "Two guineas; that's a great, great deal. If I worked, and worked, and worked ever so hard, I could no ways earn two guineas before Monday fortnight. Could I, mother?"

"Oh, no! child, no; not if you worked yourself to death."

"But I could earn something, though, I say," cried Jem proudly; "and I *will* earn something—if it be ever so little it will be *something*—and I shall do my best; that I will."

BRAVE JEM.—Part II.

Dis-heart′-ened	Cour′-age	Ap-prov′-al
Mis′-tress	Ter′-ri-ble	Lit′-ter
Scheme	En′-ter-prise	Whis′-tling
Im-pos-si-bil′-i-ties	Pro′-ject	Lei′-sure
Fail′-ures	Ac-com′-plished	Hand′-i-work
Per-se-vered′	Ex-pec-ta′-tion	Dif′-fi-cul-ty

Jem was up betimes in the morning, and soon he was on his way to the town in search of something to do. After trying hard, but in vain, he was becoming downcast and disheartened for poor Lightfoot's sake. But he gathered up courage to make another effort, and offered his services to a lady who was overlooking a gardener at work on her grounds. She was pleased with the manner of the lad, and luckily enough engaged him on trial at sixpence a day. Jem worked on bravely, and secured the approval of the gardener as well as the good graces of his mistress.

After some days the gardener asked him to stay a little while over time to help him to carry some geranium pots into the hall. Jem, always active and obliging, readily stayed from play, and was carrying in a heavy flower-pot, when his mistress crossed the hall. "What a terrible litter," said she, "you are making here; why don't you wipe your shoes upon the mat?" Jem turned round to look for the mat, but he saw none. "Oh!" said the lady, recollecting herself, "I can't blame you for there is no mat." "No, ma'am," said the gardener, "and I don't know when, if ever, the man will bring home those mats you bespoke." "I am very sorry to hear that," said the lady; "I wish we could find somebody who would do them, if *he* can't. I should not care what sort of mats they were, so that one could wipe one's feet." Jem, as he was sweeping away the litter, when he heard this, said to himself, "Perhaps I could make a mat."

All the way home, as he trudged along whistling, he was thinking over a scheme for making mats, which, however bold it may appear, he did not despair of carrying out, with patience and industry. Many were the difficulties which he foresaw; but he felt within him that spirit which spurs men on to great enterprises, and makes them "trample on impossibilities."

He recollected, in the first place, that he had seen Lazy Lawrence, the matmaker, whilst he lounged upon the gate, twist a bit of heath into different shapes; and he thought that if he could find some way of plaiting heath firmly together, it would make a very pretty, green, soft mat, which would do very well for one to wipe one's shoes on. About a mile from his mother's house, on the common which Jem rode over when he went to farmer Truck's for the giant strawberries, he remembered to have seen a great quantity of this heath; and as it was now only six o'clock in the evening, he knew that he should have time to feed Lightfoot, groom him, go to the common, return, and make one trial of his skill before he went to bed.

Lightfoot carried him swiftly to the common, and there Jem gathered as much of the heath as he thought he should want. But what toil, what time, what pains did it cost him, before he could make anything like a mat! Twenty times he was ready to throw aside the heath, and give up his project, from impatience of repeated failures. But he still persevered. Nothing truly great can be accomplished without toil and time.

Two hours he worked before he went to bed. All his leisure the next day he spent at his mat; which in all made five hours of fruitless attempts. The sixth, however, repaid him for the labours of the other five; he conquered his grand difficulty of fastening the heath firmly together, and at length completely finished a mat which far surpassed his most hopeful expectations. He was extremely happy, sung, danced round his handiwork, whistled, looked at it again and again, and could hardly leave off admiring it when it was time to go to bed. He laid it by his bed-side, that he might see it the moment he awoke in the morning.

BRAVE JEM.—Part III.

In-ge-nu′-i-ty	Jour′-neys	Com′-pa-ny
In′-dus-try	Piled	Cir′-cle
Fa′-vour	Ap-pear′-ance	Earn′-ings
Eight′-een	Gen′-tle-man	Shil′-lings
Sat′-ur-day	O-ver-whelmed′	Thir′-ty-six
Fin′-ished	Dis-ap-peared′	Coun′-te-nance

And now came the grand pleasure of carrying the mat to his mistress. The lady was surprised when she heard who made it. After having admired it, she told him not to waste his time in weeding gardens. "You can employ yourself much better," said she, "and shall have the reward of your ingenuity as well as of your industry. Make as many more such mats as you can, and I will take care and dispose of them for you." "Thank ye, ma'am," said Jem, making his best bow, for he saw by the lady's looks that she meant to do him a favour, though he repeated to himself, "'Dispose of them;' what does that mean?"

The next day he set to work to make more mats, and soon learned to make them so well and quickly, that he was surprised at his own success. In every one he made, he found less difficulty, so that instead of making two, he could soon make four, in a day. In a fortnight he made eighteen. It was Saturday night when he finished, and he carried, at three journeys, his eighteen mats to his mistress's house; piled them all up in the hall, and laid his cap on it. He stood proudly beside the pile, waiting for the lady's appearance.

Presently a folding-door at one end of the hall opened, and he saw his mistress, with a great many gentlemen and ladies, rising from several tables.

"Oh! there is my little boy with his mats," cried the lady; and, followed by all the rest of the company, she came into the hall. Jem modestly retired whilst they looked at his mats; but in a minute or two his mistress beckoned him; and when he came into the middle of the circle he saw that his pile of mats had disappeared.

"Well," said the lady, smiling, "what do you see that makes you look so surprised?" "That all my mats are gone," said Jem. "Well," said the lady, "take up your cap, and go home then, for you see that it is getting late, and you know Lightfoot will wonder what has become of you." Jem turned round to take up his cap, which he had left on the floor.

But how his countenance changed!—the cap was heavy with shillings. Every one who had taken a mat had put in two shillings; so that for the eighteen mats he had got thirty-six shillings. "Thirty-six shillings!" said the lady; "five and sevenpence I think you told me you had earned already—how much does that make? We must add one other sixpence to make out your two guineas." "Two guineas!" cried he, "Oh Lightfoot! —oh mother!"

Jem ran home to carry his earnings to his mother; and the poor widow was overwhelmed with wonder and delight. Then flying to the stable: "Lightfoot you're not to be sold to-morrow! old fellow," said he, patting him caressingly.

Miss Edgeworth.

THE IDIOT.

It had pleased God to form poor Ned
  A thing of idiot mind,
Yet to the poor unreasoning lad
  God had not been unkind.

Old Sarah loved her helpless son,
  Whom helplessness made dear;
And life was happiness to one
  Who had nor hope nor fear.

She knew his wants, she understood
  Each half-articulate call;
And he was everything to her,
  And she to him was all.

And so for many a year they dwelt,
  Nor knew a wish beside;
But age at length on Sarah came,
  And she fell sick and died.

He tried in vain to waken her,
  And called her o'er and o'er;
They told him she was dead:—the sound
  To him no import bore.

They closed her eyes and shrouded her,
  And he stood wondering by,
And when they bore her to the grave,
  He followed silently.

They laid her in the narrow house,
  They sung the funeral stave;
But when the funeral train dispersed,
  He loitered by the grave.

The rabble boys, who used to jeer,
Where'er they saw poor Ned,
Now stood and watched him at the grave,
And not a word they said.

They came and went, and came again,
Till night at last came on;
And still he loitered by the grave
Till all the rest were gone.

And when he found himself alone,
He soon removed the clay,
And raised the coffin up in haste,
And bore it swift away.

And when he reached his hut, he laid
The coffin on the floor,
And with the eagerness of joy,
He barred the cottage-door.

And out he took his mother's corse,
And placed it in a chair,
And then he heaped the hearth, and blev
The kindling fire with care.

And pausing, now her hand would feel,
And now her face behold;
"Why, mother, do you look so pale?
And why are you so cold?"

It had pleased God from the poor lad
His only friend to call;
But God was kind to him, and soon,
In death restored him all.

Southey.

THE LAST NIGHT OF THE YEAR.

Lone′-ly	Whirl′-ing	Hol′-i-days
Sor′-row-ful	Fur′-ni-ture	Christ′-mas
Mem′-o-ry	Pet′-u-lant	Three′-score
Com-pan′-ions	Dag′-gers	Sick′-ness
Re-lig′-ious	Ru′-ined	Fa-mil′-iar

On the last night of the year, an old man was sitting in his house alone, and very sorrowful. It was a wild and stormy night, and the house was a lonely one. But it was not the storm which made him sad, nor the lonely house, nor the last night of the year. The old man began to think of his past life; and as he thought and thought, with his face between his hands, the tears might be seen falling from his eyes. His early days came into his memory—the happy, sunny time of boyhood—the old house and its trees—his school days and school companions; and as he remembered them, he said bitterly, "Oh! time, time!—lost time!—but it is now too late to recall thee! When a boy, I thought old age would never come. When my parents and friends implored me to seek God early, I used, like a fool, to say, 'Time enough!' How good and happy I might have been now—how ready to meet sickness and death—if I had only begun to be religious when young. But I was ruined by ever saying, 'Time enough!' and now old age has come, and I am without hope."

The old man rose from his seat, and gazed from the window upon the dreary scene without. The snow still fell in thick and whirling flakes, and the wind roared through the leafless trees. "Dreary—dreary like my past life," said the old man; and returned to his seat beside the fire. His early friends rose up before his mind. He saw his dear father as he used to be long ago; his mother looked at him with the loving look she ever had;

he saw, too, his brothers and sisters—their merry voices rung in his ear; he saw the familiar room in his early home, and its furniture; and the very old pony and dog came before his mind. "All gone!—all gone!" he sobbed out bitterly. "Parents, sisters, brothers, are all sleeping in the old churchyard, with the snows of many winters on their graves." And then how lone his heart felt as he remembered the many times he had pained his parents—the unkind or petulant words he had spoken—the selfish things he had done. These were all daggers to him now. His brothers and sisters seemed to reproach him for not having been more kind to them while alive. "All gone!" he said, "and I here a lonely old man! Fool—fool! not to have loved them more, and done more to please them. Oh, time, time!—lost time!"

With eyes dim with tears, and a heart that seemed to burn like a coal, he again went to the window. There was a lull in the storm, the snow had ceased to fall, and the moon and stars were beginning to shine out from the breaking clouds. The old man became more soothed as he gazed on the calm, blue sky; yet he could not banish his heavy sorrow. "I fear," he said, "my last days are come; and the work which should have been begun threescore years ago, can never, never, be done. O time! time! could I but recall it, how should I labour, by God's grace, to improve it; so that when old age came, it might be like yonder sky, calm and cloudless! I would give ten thousand worlds to be young again?"

As he thus spoke, everything began to fade from his sight; the trees, the snow, the moon, all disappeared; strange light began to flash on his eyes; happy voices, as of old, rang in his ears; then a face came near his—it seemed his mother's—and near it was his father's also; he felt warm kisses on his cheek, and he heard these words breathed in his ear,—"A good new year to you, darling boy! and may God bless you, and make you his own child!" It is indeed, his mother who kisses him, and his father who blesses him; and his brothers and sisters now crowd round him, wishing him a happy new year. For the boy was at home from school during the Christmas holidays, and had been only *dreaming* that he was an old man. He awoke, and could have wept for joy when he found it was all a dream. The very old dog, as he wagged his tail and put his paws up on his bed, looking in his face, made him happy. He did not forget his dream; and by God's blessing he was enabled so to spend his youth and his riper years, that it never became in his case anything more than a dream.

Rev. Norman Macleod.

THE MOSSES.—Part I.

Dare′-say	Wil′-der-ness	Sep′-a-rate
Re-gard′-less	Hab-i-ta′-tion	Cov′-er-let
Re-vive′	Trav′-el-ler	Com′-fort-a-ble
Im-mense′	Lap′-land-ers	E-las′-tic
Mi-nute′	Cra′-dle	Af′-ri-can
Veg-e-ta′-tion	In-ter-wov′-en	Car′-pet

I daresay you have often noticed how gay the little mosses look in the winter time, when snow is on the ground, and the flowers have all hidden themselves beneath the earth, waiting for the spring to come, before they dare venture to peep forth. Every wall is covered with their bright green and yellow tufts, and they spread out their leaves, regardless of cloud and storm. But when summer comes, and the sun grows hot, the little moss dries up and withers; for though it will bear any amount of cold, it cannot live without a great deal of moisture. For some months it remains black and lifeless, until the damp and rain of autumn revive it, and make it bloom again as gay as ever.

No part of the globe appears to be entirely without mosses, and they afford shelter to an immense number of insects, protecting them, lest they should be destroyed by the frosts of winter, or parched by the heat of summer, or decayed by the damps of autumn. So that we may be assured that not even the most minute vegetable has been made in vain.

The sight of a little moss, growing in the depth of the wilderness, far away from any human habitation, was once the means of restoring the courage of Mungo Park, the famous African traveller.

In the cold and dreary country of Lapland there are not so many flowers as in Britain, but moss is very plentiful, and the Laplanders use it for a great number of purposes. They line their babies' cradles with it, and stuff it into their boats and gloves to keep the cold out; and when they want to make themselves a bed, they cut a large piece of moss from the ground, and separate it carefully from the mould. The roots are so interwoven with each other, that they do not separate, and the Laplanders can roll it up like a carpet and carry it under their arm. This mossy bed is very soft and light; and if a piece of it be used as a coverlet, nothing can be more warm and comfortable. If after a time it gets too dry and withered, they have only to dip it into water, and it becomes as fresh and elastic as before.

THE MOSSES.—PART II.

In-debt′-ed	De-li′-cious	Scant′-y
Re-al′-ity	Re-course′	Blos′-som
Lich′-en	Dan′-ger-ous	Des′-o-late
Pro-fu′-sion	Flour′-ish	Mead′-ows
Rein′-deer	Nour′-ish-ment	Cat′-tle
Fod′-der	Ver′-dure	Ben′-e-fit-ed

The Laplanders are also very much indebted to another little plant called the "reindeer moss" but which is in reality a lichen. It grows in the utmost profusion, covering vast plains, hundreds of miles in extent; and being of a whitish color, it looks like snow upon the ground. These plains would appear to us, who live in a brighter land, to be mere dry and barren wastes, but to the Laplanders they are rich and fertile fields; for when the cold of winter has frozen up every herb and blade of grass, and driven man and beasts to the shelter of the vallies and the woods, this moss becomes the sole food of the herds of reindeer, which form the chief wealth of the Laplanders.

Nor is this all. During the rainy season when the moss is very soft and easily separated from the ground, the Laplanders rake it together in heaps, and use it as fodder for their cows. In these cold regions, I must tell you that the cows are no larger than calves, but their milk is almost all cream, and sweeter and more delicious than any one can imagine, The reason is that they feed so much upon the reindeer moss.

There is another little plant, called the "Iceland moss," which is also a lichen, and is used as food by the inhabitants of Iceland.

These poor people rarely obtain corn bread, and their stock of provisions is so scanty, that they are obliged to have recourse to every kind of vegetable they can procure.

The Iceland moss consists of upright leaves, nearly two inches high, soft and pliant when they are moist; but hardened and rigid when dry. They are smooth and shining, of a red colour towards the root, and the outer surface is sprinkled with very small black warts.

The plant is collected by the Icelanders, and after being washed and dried in the sun, it is put into a bag and well beaten. Last of all it is worked into a powder by being trampled upon, and then it is ready to be used for making bread.

Small as the mosses are, they are of so much use to man, that they have been called his servants or workmen, and I will tell you in what way they serve him best.

They will often sow themselves on the surface of a bog, or piece of loose wet ground, where it is dangerous to tread; but in course of time, they will hold the soil together, and make it quite safe.

Another use of the mosses is more striking still.

Picture to yourself a barren rock on which nothing has ever grown, and to look at it you would not suppose that either trees or flowers could ever flourish upon it. But by and bye some seeds of moss are wafted thither by the winds. They do not require any soil to grow in, for they draw their nourishment from the air; so they strike root, and soon cover the rock with verdure. When summer comes, they wither and die, but they leave behind a thin layer of soil, ready for more seeds to sow themselves in. Ages pass away, and every year the mosses come and make the soil a little deeper. Then other plants begin to grow, flowers spring up and blossom, and the rock does not look desolate any longer. Men begin to sow corn upon it; there are meadows for cattle to feed in; woods and forests clothe it with beauty; and thus by the labours of a little moss, mankind is benefited, and barren places made rich and fruitful.

The Observing Eye.

THE RIVER.

River, river, little river!
Bright you sparkle on your way,
O'er the yellow pebbles dancing,
Through the flowers and foliage glancing,—
Like a child at play.

River, river, swelling river!
On you rush o'er rough and smooth,
Louder, faster, rolling, leaping,
Over rocks and shallows sweeping,—
Like impetuous youth.

River, river, brimming river!
Broad, and deep, and still as time,
Seeming still, although in motion,
Tending onward to the ocean,—
Just like mortal prime.

River, river, rapid river!
Swifter now you slip away,
Swift and silent as an arrow,
Through a channel dark and narrow,—
Like life's closing day.

River, river, headlong river!
Down you dash into the sea,—
Sea, that line hath never sounded,
Sea, that sail hath never rounded,—
Like eternity.

Mrs. Southey.

THE CROCUS'S SONG.

Down in my solitude under the snow,
  Where nothing cheering can reach me;
Here, without light to see how to grow,
  I'll trust to nature to teach me.

I will not despair, nor be idle nor frown,
  Locked in so gloomy a dwelling;
My leaves shall run up, and my roots shall run down,
  While the bud in my bosom is swelling.

Soon as the frost will get out of my bed,
  From this cold dungeon to free me,
I will peer up with my little bright head:
  All will be joyful to see me.

Then from my heart will young petals diverge
  As rays of the sun from their focus;
I from the darkness of earth will emerge,
  A happy and beautiful Crocus!

Many, perhaps, from so simple a flower
  This little lesson may borrow,—
Patient to-day, through its gloomiest hour,
  We come out the brighter to-morrow.

Gould.

SECTION III.

NATURAL HISTORY.

THE RAT WITH A BELL.

A FABLE.

In-fest′-ed	Re-cov′-er-y	Mop′-ing
Dep-re-da′-tion	Sus-pect′-ing	Laugh′-ing
Pro-tec′-tion	Ri′-ot-ed	Earn′-est-ly
Wain′-scots	Pleas′-ant-ly	So-ci′-e-ty
Stragg′-ler	Diff′-i-cul-ty	Sol′-i-tar-y
Coll′-ar	Dis-con′-so-late	Af-fec′-tion

A large old house in the country was so extremely infested with rats, that nothing could be secured from their depredations. They scaled the walls to attack flitches of bacon, though hung as high as the ceiling. Hanging shelves afforded no protection to the cheese and pastry. They found their way into the store-room, and plundered it of preserves and sweetmeats. They gnawed through cupboard doors, undermined floors, and ran races behind the wainscots. The cats could not get at them: they were too cunning and too well fed to meddle with poison; and traps only now and then caught a heedless straggler. One of these, however, on being taken, was the occasion of practising a new device. This was, to fasten a collar with a small bell about the prisoner's neck, and then turn him loose again.

Overjoyed at the recovery of his liberty the rat ran into the nearest hole, and went in search of his companions. They heard at a distance the bell tinkle, tinkle, through the dark passage, and suspecting some enemy had got among them, away they scoured, some one way, and some another. The bell-bearer pursued, and soon guessing the cause of their flight, he was greatly amused by it. Wherever he approached, it was all hurry-scurry, and not a tail of one of them was to be seen. He chased his old friends from hole to hole, and room to room, laughing all the while at their fears, and increasing them by all the means in his power. Presently he had the whole house to himself. "That's right," quoth he, "the fewer, the better cheer." So he rioted alone among the good things, and stuffed himself till he could hardly walk.

For two or three days this course of life went on very pleasantly. He ate and ate, and played the bugbear to perfection. At length he grew tired of this lonely condition, and longed to mix with his companions again upon the former footing. But the difficulty was how to get rid of his bell. He pulled and tugged with his forefeet, and almost tore the skin off his neck in the attempt, but all in vain. The bell was now his plague and torment. He wandered from room to room, earnestly desiring to make himself known tc one of his companions, but they all kept out of his reach. At last as he was moping about disconsolate, he fell in puss's way, and was devoured in an instant.

He who is raised so much above his fellow-creatures as to be the object of their terror, must suffer for it in losing all the comforts of society. He is a solitary being in the midst of crowds. He keeps them at a distance, and they equally shun him. Dread and affection cannot subsist together.

Evenings at Home.

THE BOY AND THE CAPTIVE BIRD.

Oh! give it liberty!
Canst thou not tell
The blessings of the free?
No! for the captive's cheerless cell
Hath never closed on thee.

Who pray for health?
They who have felt
Disease's weary bed.
Who pine for wealth?
They who have knelt,
And vainly begg'd for bread.

Then give it liberty!
Blue sky and balmy breeze,
And shelter of the greenwood tree,
Oh! how it droops for these!

True, thou hast made its home
Of gaily-gilded bars;
But what are these to heaven's free dome
With all its twinkling stars?

Think ye the captive's brain
Could grow to slavery cold,
Though every limb might wear a chain
Of brightly-burnished gold?

Then give it liberty!
For thee 'tis well
Thy glad young life is free.
Pray that the solitary cell
May never close on thee!

J. A.

THE SADDLER'S PET RAT.

Leath'-er	Nibb'-ling	Lei'-sure-ly
O-rig'-in-al	Be-hav'-iour	Ac-com'-pa-ny
Brit'-ish	Tol'-er-ab-ly	De-struc'-tion
Dain'-ty	A'-pron	In-quis'-it-ive-ly
Van'-ished	As-ton'-ish-ment	Per-form'-ance
Sadd'-ler	In'-no-cent	Un-fort'-u-nate
Pris'-on-er	Break'-fast	Mur'-der-ous

I knew a worthy whipmaker who worked hard at his trade to support a large family. He had prepared a number of strips of leather, by well-oiling and greasing them. These he carefully laid by in a box, but, strange to say, they disappeared one by one: nobody knew anything about them, nobody had touched them.

However, one day as he was sitting at work in his shop, a large black rat of the original British kind, slyly poked his head out of a hole in the corner of the room, and coolly took a look about the place. Seeing all quiet, out he came, and ran straight to the box in which were kept the favourite leather strips. In he dived, and quickly re-appeared, carrying in his mouth the most dainty morsel he could find. Off he ran to his hole, and vanished.

Having thus found out the thief, the saddler determined to catch him. He accordingly propped up a sieve with a stick, and put a bait underneath. In a few minutes out came the rat again, smelling the inviting toasted cheese, and forthwith attacked it. The moment he began nibbling at the bait, down came the sieve, and he became a prisoner. "Now," thought he, "my life depends upon my behaviour, when this horrid sieve is lifted up by that two-legged monster with the apron. He has a tolerably good-natured face, and I don't think he wants to kill me. I know what to do."

The whipmaker at length lifted up the sieve, being armed with a stick ready to kill Mr. Rat when he rushed out. What was his astonishment on seeing that he remained perfectly still. After a few moments he walked quietly up the whipmaker's arm, and looked up in his face, as much as to say, "I am a poor innocent rat, and if your wife *will* lock up all the good things in the cupboard, why I must eat your nice thongs. Rats must live as well as whipmakers."

The man then said, "Tom, I was going to kill you, but now I won't; let us be friends. I'll give you some bread and butter every day if you will not take my thongs and wax, and leave the shopman's breakfast alone. But I am afraid you will come out once too often—there are lots of dogs and cats about who won't be so civil to you."

He then put him down, and Mr. Rat leisurely retired to his hole. For a long time afterwards he found his breakfast regularly placed for him at the mouth of his hole; in return for which he, as in duty bound, became quite tame, running about the shop, and inquisitively turning over everything on the bench at which his protector was at work. He would even accompany him into the stables when he went to feed the pony; and pick up the corn as it fell from the manger, keeping however, a respectful distance from the pony's legs. His chief delight was to bask on the warm window-sill in the mid-day sun. This comfortable but unfortunate habit proved his destruction, for one very hot day as he lay taking his nap, the dog belonging to the bird-shop opposite spied him afar off, and instantly dashed at him through the window. The poor rat, who was asleep at the time, awoke, alas! too late to save his life. The dog caught him, and took him into the road, where a few sharp squeezes and shakings soon finished him.

The fatal deed being done, the murderous dog left his bleeding victim in the dusty road, and, with ears and tail erect, walked away quite proud of his performance.

Curiosities of Nat. Hist.

THE CROW OF CEYLON.

Cey-lon'	At-tract'-ed	Im-me'-di-ate-ly
Gloss'-y	At-ten'-tion	Ar-ri'-val
Sen'-si-ble	Ev'-i-dent-ly	Doubt'-less
En-gag'-ing	Op-por-tu'-nit-y	In'-sult
Gov'-ern-or	Baf'-fled	Lib'-er-ty

In the island of Ceylon there is to be found a very cunning and sensible crow, somewhat smaller than our own native one, having a glossy back, and altogether rather an engaging pretty bird. Now, in the yard of the Governor of Ceylon, a dog was one day amusing himself by gnawing a bone, the scraps of meat upon which attracted the attention of one of these crows. It alighted on the ground, hopped round the dog and the bone, and evidently waited for an opportunity of seizing the latter. The dog, however, was on his guard, and by certain growls and probably angry looks, which the bird understood, no doubt, protected his property. The crow was too cunning and too hungry to be baffled. He flew away, but soon returned with a companion. They hopped up to the dog, when the fresh arrival watched his opportunity and gave a sudden pull at the dog's tail. Not being used to such an insult he suddenly turned round, in order to see who had taken this liberty with him. The bone was for a moment left unprotected, and was immediately seized by the first cunning crow, who flew away with it, joined by his companion, and they doubtless had a merry feast upon it.

Edward Jesse.

THE OWL.

Why dost thou wander, lonesome owl,
Now everything beside, each fowl
And beast, to rest is laid?
Why do thy broad wings shine so bright,
From mead to mead, when the dim night
Bids all the prospect fade?

Doth the sun blind thine eyes by day,
That, hid from sight, thou steal'st away
Amid the ivy tree?
Go, silly owl, go, sleep till morn,
Shall to the woods and fields return,
Then wake and sport like me.

"Ah! little boy," the owl would say,
"How dost thou know how blythe and gay
I hail the twilight hour.
When the pale stars are up, then I
Am out beneath their gentle sky,
The mistress of the bower.

When lark and linnet lie asleep
In their warm nest, 'tis then I keep
My merry-makings here:
My hootings long and loud, no less
Than their sweet songs can joy express,
And my companions cheer.

The moon sheds down her brightest beams,
To guide me by the woods and streams,
Home to my dark old tree;
And when the sun brings back his joys,
Then little birds and little boys,
In turn may merry be."

Pretty Poems.

SPIDERS.

Ex-am'-ine	In'-dus-try	Ab-do'-men
Stubb'-le	Lob'-sters	Mi'-cro-scope
Em-ploy'-ment	Ma-ter'-i-als	Re-bell'-ious
Ac-tiv'-i-ty	Prop'-er-ty	Con'-quer-or
En'-er-gy	E-las-tic'-i-ty	Wa-'ry
Per-se-ver'-ance	Thor'-ax	Pin'-cers

If we wish to find spiders, we must peep into dusty holes and corners in stables, barns, and houses. We must ramble in the garden and search amongst shrubs. We must look into rolled-up leaves, into the cups of flowers, into holes in stones, and holes in the ground; we must examine brick walls—we must look carefully, and step lightly over the dewy grass and the fresh stubble field, and if we mount a high church steeple, we shall perchance see spiders sailing in the air still higher above us. If we looked far down into the clear water of some ponds and ditches, we might perhaps see a spider all alive, comfortably nestled in a bright silvery house of her own preparing. She has filled her little house with air, and fastened it down by silken cords. to the quiet green leaves at the bottom of the pond.

If we notice the habits of these spiders, we shall find that some can run, some can leap, and some can fly on streamers of silk of their own spinning; that some lay snares, and others hide in ambush. We shall find they follow different employments ; that some are weavers, some are tent-makers, some are masons, and some are carpenters.

During the winter, spiders are sleepy and dull; but for the greater part of the year they are busily employed in catching their food, and in tenderly caring for, and rearing their young. In all they do, spiders show great activity, energy, perseverance, and industry; and display so much skill that they may truly be said to be most wonderful little creatures.

A spider is a jointed animal. Around its soft body are many horny rings or hoops; these in some parts are joined together by a tough skin to form joints, and in other parts they are pressed so closely to one another, that they make a firm case. The rings of crabs and lobsters are formed of hard lime or chalk, but the rings of a spider are softer, being made of more horny materials. And when horn is there, it possesses the property of elasticity, or slightly yielding with a spring. Spiders have no gills; some kinds have two, and others eight holes in their sides, through which they breathe. These holes open into little tubes that take the air down into sacs or bags in the body. The inside of these tubes is lined with a skin that folds over in plaits, and these plaits are full of little veins that take in the air for the purpose of being mixed with the blood.

Did you ever remark, as a spider ran past you, that its body was divided into two parts? The front part is called the thorax, or breast. The thorax is the hardest part of the body; and all the principal organs of the spider, such as its head and legs, are fastened to it. The other part of the spider's body is soft, and only covered with a thick skin; this is called the abdomen; it contains the stomach, the air sacs, and the bags of gummy silk from which the spider makes its threads. These front and hinder parts are joined together by a slender tube.

The legs of spiders are rather long. You know how fine a spider's leg looks; and yet this fine leg is jointed, and has several strong muscles, or little cords running down each of its sides. These muscles give the spider power to move quickly and to hold tightly; and they also enable it to lift its body from the ground and to keep it steady upon its many-jointed legs. The worm has no legs; crabs and lobsters scrape their stout limbs slowly along, and lay them close to the ground; but the tight trim legs of the spider stand up, and are as tough as wire, and in their action as nimble as thought.

The spider has jaw-feet on its head. In some spiders a few of these jaw-feet are tipped with sharp hooks; and in other spiders they are tipped with pincers, resembling crab's claws. The microscope shows us, that at the end of these hooks or pincers there is a little hole, from out of which flows at will a drop of poison, and this enters the wound it has pricked in any captured insect. When a fly is caught, the spider runs along the fine threads of its web, darts his hook or pincers into the body, and then goes away In a few minutes, and sometimes in a few moments, this poison kills the fly.

If the spider finds that a large fly is caught, and fears that its bouncing will break the web, it quickly bites through the threads that are close to the fly, and lets it go away. But if another fly, not quite so large, tries to fight the spider with its legs and wings, then the wary fellow spins a little more web out of its own body, and throws these threads over the fly. When it finds that tbis silken cordage has well bound down the rebellious captive, off it runs to some quiet corner, and there waits till the poor fly has fairly tired itself out with struggling; and as soon as it has become quiet, the watchful spider runs along the net, and darts its jaw-feet into its body. The poison shortly kills the prisoner; and then the conqueror comes back, and lifting the fly out of the web, carries it away to dine upon it in a snug corner close by.

Observing Eye.

THE SPIDER AND THE FLY.

A NEW VERSION OF AN OLD STORY.

Will you walk into my parlour ?" said the Spider to the Fly;
Tis the prettiest little parlour that ever you did spy.
e way into my parlour is up a winding stair,
d I have many curious things to show when you are there."
Oh no, no," said the little Fly, " to ask me is in vain,
r who goes up your winding stair can ne'er come down again."

'm sure you must be weary, dear, with soaring up so high;
ill you rest upon my little bed ?" said the Spider to the Fly.
There are pretty curtains drawn around; the sheets are fine and thin,
d if you like to rest awhile, I'll snugly tuck you in !"
Oh no, no," said the little Fly, " for I've often heard it said,
ey never, never wake again, who sleep upon your bed !"

id the cunning Spider to the Fly, " Dear friend, what can I do,
prove the warm affection I've always felt for you ?
ave within my pantry good store of all that's nice ;
n sure you're very welcome—will you please to take a slice ?"
Oh no, no," said the little Fly, " kind sir that cannot be,
e heard what's in your pantry, and I do not wish to see !"

" Sweet creature !" said the Spider, " you're witty and you're wise ;
How handsome are your gauzy wings ! how brilliant are your eyes !
I have a little looking-glass upon my parlour shelf,
If you'll step in one moment, dear, you shall behold yourself."
" I thank you, gentle sir," she said, " for what you're pleased to say,
And bidding you good morning now, I'll call another day."

The Spider turn'd him round about, and went into his den,
For well he knew the silly Fly would soon come back again ;
So he wove a subtle web in a little corner sly,
And set his table ready, to dine upon the Fly.
Then he came out to his door again, and merrily did sing—
" Come hither, hither, pretty Fly, with the pearl and silver wing ;
Your robes are green and purple ; there's a crest upon your head ;
Your eyes are like the diamond bright, but mine are dull as lead !"

Alas, alas ! how very soon this silly little Fly,
Hearing his wily flattering words, came slowly flitting by ;
With buzzing wings she hung aloft, then near and nearer drew,
Thinking only of her brilliant eyes, and green and purple hue ;
Thinking only of her crested head ; poor foolish thing ! At last—

Up jump'd the cunning Spider, and fiercely held her
fast;
He dragg'd her up his winding stair, into his dismal
den—
Within his little parlour—but she ne'er came out again!

And now, dear little children, who may this story read,
To idle, silly, flattering words, I pray you ne'er give
heed;
Unto an evil counsellor, close heart and ear and eye,
And take a lesson from this tale of the Spider and the
Fly.

Mary Howitt.

THE DOG.

Em-ploy'-ments	Sa-gac'-i-ty	E-spec'-ial-ly
Ea'-ger-ness	Pe-cul'-iar	In-tel'-li-gent
Es-sen'-tial	Del'-i-cate	Cour-a'-geous
Pe'-ri-od	Do-cil'-i-ty	Sa-ga'-cious
Lit'-er-a-ture	Be-nev'-o-lence	Res-o-lu'-tion

The dog stands to man in the relation both of a valuable servant and an engaging companion. In many employments, especially those of shepherds and herdsmen, he performs services of great importance, such as could not be supplied without him. In those sports of the field, such as hunting and shooting, which many persons pursue with such eagerness, the assistance of the dog is essential to success. By his keenness of scent he discovers the game, and by his swiftness of foot he runs it down. There is no period of time recorded by history in which we do not find the dog the friend and the servant of man; nor is there any literature which does not contain some tribute to his faithfulness and sagacity.

A long course of taming, and peculiar modes of

breeding and rearing, have divided the canine race into nearly a hundred varieties, many of which show marked difference in size and appearance. The savage bull-dog seems hardly to belong to the same race as the delicate lap-dog, that sleeps on the rug, and is washed and combed by its fair mistress almost as carefully as an infant. The swift and slim greyhound looks very little like the sturdy and square-built mastiff. But there are certain marks of character, which, in a greater or less degree, are common to all the kinds. Sagacity, docility, benevolence, a capacity to receive instruction, and attachment to his master's person, are qualities which belong to the whole race.

Many instances have been recorded in which persons have been saved from drowning by dogs, especially by those of the Newfoundland breed, which have a natural love for the water.—A vessel was once driven by a storm on the beach, in the county of Kent, in England. Eight men were calling for help, but not a boat could be got off to their assistance. At length a gentleman came on the beach accompanied by his Newfoundland dog. He directed the attention of the noble animal to the vessel, and put a short stick into his mouth. The intelligent and courageous dog at once understood his meaning, and sprang into the sea, fighting his way through the foaming waves. He could not, however, get close enough to the vessel to deliver that with which he was charged, but the crew joyfully made fast a rope to another piece of wood, and threw it towards him. The sagacious dog saw the whole business in an instant, he dropped his own piece and immediately seized that which had been cast to him; and then, with a degree of strength and resolution almost incredible, he dragged it through the surge, and delivered it to his master. By this means a line of communication was formed, and every man on board saved.

THE SHEPHERD'S DOG.

Shrewd	**Dis-tin′-guish**	**Ex-pres′-sion**
Va-ri′-e-ty	**Po-ta′-toes**	**Pas′-tu-rage**
Mar′-vel-lous	**In-trud′-ers**	**Or′-di-na-ry**
Quar′-rel-some	**Com′-i-cal**	**Com-mu′-ni-ca-ting**
Thieves	**Span′-iel**	**Ca-ress′-es**

This variety of the dog can equally bear the heat of summer and the cold of winter. He does not mix with other dogs than those of his own race, or with other men than those whom he is destined to serve. His powers of instinct are directed to one object, and like his master he is shrewd, prompt, and observant. His eye, often overshadowed by shaggy hair, is bright and sparkling: he understands every signal; he obeys on the instant, and manages his work with marvellous tact and quickness. This done, he returns quietly to his master with the air of one conscious of having done his duty.

The shepherd's dog is of middle stature, or rather low in proportion to his length; he is slightly formed, and quick and active in his movements. Though not quarrelsome, he is very courageous, and will resolutely encounter the fox in defence of the sheep; and though unlike the spaniel, he is indifferent to caresses, and distant towards strangers, yet to his master he is most devotedly attached When the labour of the day is over, —when the sheep are folded for the night,—he returns with him home to the humble cottage and there curls up underneath his master's chair, or sits by his side and partakes of his simple repast.

It is an interesting sight to see a clever dog turn a flock of wild black-faced sheep in whichever direction his master wishes. He makes a wide sweep to get round the sheep without frightening them; and having got beyond them, he then rushes barking from flank to flank of the flock, and brings them all up in close array to the desired spot. When, too, the shepherd wishes to catch a particular sheep out of the flock, I have seen him point it out to the dog, who would instantly distinguish it from the rest, and follow it up till caught. I have been with a shepherd when he has ordered his dog to drive a part of the flock home,—the man remaining with me on the hill. On our return we always found that the dog had either given up his charge to the shepherd's wife, or had driven the sheep without assistance into the fold, himself lying down at the narrow entrance to keep them from getting out till his master came home. At other times I have seen a dog keeping watch on the hill over a flock of sheep, allowing them to feed all day, but always keeping sight of them, and bringing them home at a proper hour in the evening.

The sheep-dog often watches his master's crop of oats or potatoes, keeping off all intruders in the shape of sheep, cattle, horses, or thieves. A shepherd once, to prove the quickness of his dog, who was lying before the fire in the house where we were talking, said to me in the middle of a sentence about something else, "I'm thinking, Sir, the cow is in the potatoes." Though he said these words in a quiet tone of voice, the dog, who seemed to be asleep, instantly jumped up and leaping through the open window, scrambled up the turf roof of the house, from which he could see the potatoe-field. Not seeing the cow there, he ran and looked into the cow-house where she was, and finding that all was right, came back to the house. After a short time the shepherd said the same words again, and the dog repeated his look-out. But on the false alarm being a third time given, the dog got up, and wagging his tail, looked his master in the face with a comical expression of inquiry. We could not help laughing at his comical look; on which, with a slight growl and an offended air, he laid himself down in his warm corner, as if determined not to be made a fool of again.

Some years since I knew a dog of this breed belonging to a farm-servant who had a large herd of cows under his charge. During the summer they were depastured on very extensive fields in Cheshire, communicating with one another. Morning and evening, at the bidding of his master, this dog would range the pasturage, bring them together, and gently drive them to the accustomed milking-place. If when he had driven them for some distance he discovered that one was missing, having wandered astray, he would run back and traverse the fields till he had met with the object of his search, which he would conduct to the herd, and then pursue his ordinary duty.

St. John, &c.

THE DOGS OF ST. BERNARD.

Per-pet′-u-al	Guar′-di-an	Per-suade′
Av′-a-lanch-es	In-tel′-li-gence	Slip′-per-y
Im-pas′-sa-ble	Val′-u-a-ble	Crack′-ling
Ex-ces′-sive	En-deav′-our-ing	Mis′-er-a-ble
Snow′-drift	Cou′-ri-er	Pied′-mont

Far up the Great St. Bernard, one of those high mountains of the Alps, which are covered with almost perpetual snow, stands a famous Convent. There the terrible avalanches often fall into the plains below, and the hollow places of the mountains, with a noise like thunder. These are great masses of snow, which hang so loosely on the sides of the mountains, that the slightest sound, which causes the air to tremble, will make them slip downwards. The traveller is often in fear, lest they should come tumbling down, and bury him in a deep snowy grave. Again, in these mountains, the snow-storms are so thick, that one's eyes get soon blinded, while the passes become so blocked up, that it is almost impossible to find the way.

"Supposing you were taking a journey across the Alps, from Switzerland into Italy, and that such a storm came on, while the night was drawing near, and you were weary with travelling, and nearly perishing with cold; what would you do?"

"I would look for the Convent of St. Bernard."

"Ah! but you are hemmed in with rocks on all sides, and the road every moment is becoming more and more impassable, and by and by every trace of it will disappear."

"I should just lie down and die."

"That is what many have done, and you would be all the more disposed to do so, because the excessive cold would make you feel overcome with sleep. The whole of your body would begin to feel numb, as your foot does when you complain that it is *asleep*, and soon you would be quite unable to go any farther.

"Well, suppose that at the very moment you were about to give all up in despair, you heard the deep baying of a dog, coming nearer and nearer, amid the darkness and snowdrift, would not that be the sweetest sound you ever heard in your life? And how thankful you would be, if, while yet able to hold on for a little, you noticed a couple of large, noble-looking dogs coming up to you—one having a flask of cordial tied to his neck, and the other, carrying a cloak to wrap around you. Would you not for one moment believe that these were the guardian spirits of the mountains, in a brute form?

"How eagerly you would untie the flask with your trembling hands, and drink! And how gratefully wrap the cloak around you! While the dogs, delighted with their success, and looking up at you with happy inteligence, would place themselves, one on either side, take ı piece of the cloak in their teeth, and so pull you along o the convent.

"Or, supposing you had already lain down and could ee or hear nothing, the dogs would at once see how natters stood. They would hasten back to fetch the nonks, who would speedily accompany them to the pot; carry you to the convent, and have you rubbed nd warmed, till the life-blood began to flow again, and ou awoke, to know that you were saved.

"Even were you buried in the snow, these noble nimals would know, by their keen sense of smell, xactly where you lay; they would scrape with their eet until your body was uncovered, and would bark oudly, endeavouring to make themselves heard; and f they did not succeed, would run for human help as ast as possible.

"One dog saved the lives of twenty-two persons, vho would have perished without his aid, and he wore ı medal round his neck, which was given him in honour of his deeds. I shall tell you the manner in which he net with his death:—

"At the foot of the mountain of St. Bernard is ituated the little village of St. Pierre; and there dwelt, ımong others, a poor courier, whose business it was to arry letters and messages across the mountain into Piednont—that part of Italy which lies at the foot of the ther side of the Alps. Well, one time, when he was on is way back to his home, it happened that one of the nost terrible storms came on which was ever known in hese regions. With great difficulty he made his way o the convent, and there the kind monks did all they ould to persuade him to remain until the storm had passed away. But the desire of seeing his family overame all the warnings of prudence. He thought they would make themselves miserable, by imagining that he had perished in the storm; and this indeed was the truth. At that very moment they were wandering about in quest of him, and were toiling up the mountain's steep, slippery sides.

"The poor man's heart told him he must proceed, and the monks spoke to him in vain. All they could do was to furnish him with two guides, attended by two dogs, one of which was the valuable animal I spoke of. But the courier and his family never met. Two avalanches were just then trembling before their fall. A crackling sound was heard; then a crash like thunder. Courier, wife, children, guides, and dogs—all found a grave under the eternal snows."

Lessons in Natural History.

THE REINDEER.

Mi'-gra-to-ry	Bar'-ri-er	Gre-ga'-ri-ous
Do-mes'-tic	Fa-tigue'	Pres-er-va'-tion
Mel'-an-chol-y	Por'-trait	Pro-ces'-sion
Sol'-i-ta-ry	Suf-fi'-cient	Per-sua'-sion
Veg'-e-ta-ble	Sep-tem'-ber	Im-plic'-it-ly
A-bun'-dant-ly	Ex-traor'-di-na-ry	Ac'-ci-dent
Prov'-en-der	Ex-er'-tions	In-fe'-ri-or

The finest reindeer are met with in Finmark, Lapland, and Spitzbergen; those of Sweden and Norway are inferior in strength and size.

The reindeer is migratory in its habits, and lives in vast herds, which travel from woods to the open hills, and back again, according to the season. The woods are their winter haunts, and here they live on the long lichen which covers the ground. When spring returns they hasten from the woods to the mountain ranges—not so much on account of food as to escape the tormenting stings of the gnat and the gadfly, which lay an egg in very wound they make. Even the domestic reindeer, the ole wealth of the Laplander, is compelled to flee away rom his lowland haunts from the same cause; and ence the Laplander, who cannot exist without him, ecomes a wanderer at this season.

Nothing can be more dreary and melancholy than the ountry of Lapland, with its desolate mountains, uncul- ivated woods, vast and solitary lakes, and plains of lry barren sand, upon which the only vegetable growth s the gray reindeer moss, or lichen. In the winter the ntense cold drives the reindeer from the mountains, and e returns to the woodland and the plains. The growth f the reindeer moss, of which there are two kinds, one elonging to the woods, the other to the mountains, is f the greatest importance, both to the reindeer and his naster, as, without it, the reindeer must perish, and with im the Laplander. But this lichen is native to the soil f Lapland, and the Laplander reckons himself rich, vhen possessed of deserts which produce this plant bundantly, for, in that case, his reindeer herds are well rovided for. No supply of hay or dried provender is eeded for them during the winter, as they search for he moss beneath the snow. Now and then, it happens, owever, that the winter sets in with rain, and a cover- ng of ice incrusts the earth before the snow falls, and he food of the reindeer is laid beneath icy barriers, from which nothing but the sun of the following spring will elease it. A famine ensues; the reindeer perish from want, and with them those who are dependent upon hem.

Without the reindeer the inhabitants of Finmark, Lapland, and the shores of the Arctic Sea could not exist. It is their beast of burden; they are sustained by its flesh and milk, and clothed in its hide. The reindeer is their wealth. A Laplander possessed of a herd of rein- deer, which consists of from three to five hundred, can live comfortably. In summer sufficient cheese is made for the family supply, and during winter he can afford to kill enough to furnish them with venison. A man with two hundred is but in middling circumstances, and with one hundred he is poor ; should he have but fifty, he joins his small herd to that of a richer man, and becomes a sort of a servant. Early in September the herds and their owners return from the mountains to their winter quarters that they may be settled down before the snow commences and the winter sets in; at which season especially the full value of the reindeer is known. He is then harnessed to the sledge; and his power and usefulness in this way are extraordinary. A single deer will draw about 250 pounds' weight, and trot at the rate of ten miles an hour; frequently, indeed, they will at one stretch go one hundred and fifty miles in about nineteen hours. There is a portrait of a reindeer in the palace at Stockholm, which, upon some very important occasion, travelled eight hundred English miles in forty-eight hours; but the poor creature paid for its exertions with its life. Arrived at the end of its journey, it dropped down dead.

Reindeer are extremely gregarious—that is fond of living in herds—and their unwillingness to part company with their fellows is often the preservation of the Laplander, who otherwise might become separated from his companions, lose his way, and perish.

In proceeding across the extensive and endless lakes of Lapland, if the number of deer be great, a long and close procession is formed; each deer following the sledge that goes before it, so that the head of the deer almost touches the shoulder of the driver before. On goes the long line of sledges keeping the exact course of the foremost one, let it wind as it may. No persuasion or force can turn any single deer aside : but this very unwillingness to part company ensures the safety of the traveller. Should, however, accident or fatigue throw e considerably in the rear, the traveller may trust tly to his faithful servant to overtake the rest by wer of his scent alone. While thus separated is companions, he appears anxious and disturbed, ntinually smells with his head close to the ground, log, to regain the track. Were it not for this ty of the reindeer, travelling across Lapland and h the mountains of Finmark would be extremely ous, especially in dark and stormy weather, for the ey wear can only be heard at a short distance.

Brooke.

THE CAMEL.

-e-da-ry	Jos′-tling	Pann′-ier
-course	Bac′-tri-an	Car′-a-van
r-ates	Stom′-achs	Re-li′-ance
-wind	Pom′-mel	Va-ri′-e-ties
han-dise	Straight′-ens	Jerked
-u-lar	Al-ter′-nate-ly	Twen′-ty

re are two varieties of the camel; the Bactrian with two hunches; and the dromedary, with one. The first is a native of Asia, and the belongs to the African continent.

camel with two hunches is much stronger and on its legs than the dromedary, and is chiefly ed as a beast of burden; its great strength enab- to carry very heavy loads. The dromedary is a ighter and more active creature, and is the chief of maintaining an intercourse between the differ- ts of Africa and Arabia. The Arab venerates nel as the gift of heaven, and without its aid he neither subsist, trade, nor travel.

hose parts of the world there are districts where n shines upon vast plains of parched and trackless sand. Sometimes a whirlwind raises this loose sand in clouds; at other times the traveller has to dread the fury of a scorching wind, called the *Simoom*. But, in all his difficulties, his reliance is on the camel; which has been called "*the Ship of the Desert*," because it is so much used to convey merchandise across those sandy plains, which would otherwise be impassable.

The camel is from five to seven feet high; the head is small, the neck very long, and the body of a long irregular shape, the legs tall and slender, and the tail reaches to the joints of the hind legs. The feet are very large, and are hoofed in a very peculiar manner. The under part of the feet is protected by a long, tough, and pliable skin, which by yielding in all directions enables the animal to travel with perfect security over dry, hot, and sandy regions.

While being laden, camels show their dislike to any packet which appears too heavy. When, however, it is once on their backs, they continue to bear it with the patient expression of countenance which I fear passes for more than it is worth. All camels are loaded kneeling, and they can go from twenty-four to sixty hours without rest, and with no more than a few mouthfuls of food, which they crop off a thorny bush as they pass; or a handful of barley given them by their master. Parts of the desert are strewed with small, dry, drab-coloured plants, thorny and otherwise, which the camels continue to crop as they walk, jostling the rider not a little.

They can go long without water, and, if one considers the parching heat of the desert, this is the more to be wondered at. It is partly, no doubt, owing to the large supply they can at one time take into, and carry in, their stomachs. I have seen camels go for eleven or twelve days without a drop of water. All of them did not drink even when we came to water, nor did any drink a large quantity or seem disturbed by the want of it, though the sun was very powerful, and we travelled twelve or thirteen hours daily.

At first they are difficult to ride. The rider mounts while the animal is kneeling, and sits like a lady, with the right leg over the fore pommel of the saddle. In rising, the camel suddenly straightens its hind legs before moving either of the fore ones, so that if the rider is unprepared he will be jerked over its ears. It moves the legs of each side alternately, which sways the rider to and fro. The motion, however, is soon learned; and, when fatigued, the rider can change sides, or shift his position in various ways.

Sometimes a traveller places his whole family, wife and children, in one pannier, fastened to the saddle; puts himself in another on the opposite side, and accompanies any caravan he happens to fall in with.

Stories of Animals.

THE CAMEL.

Camel, thou art good and mild,
Docile as a little child;
Thou wast made for usefulness,
Man to comfort and to bless:
Thou dost clothe him; thou dost feed
Thou dost lend to him thy speed;
And through wilds of trackless sand,
In the hot Arabian land,
Where no rock its shadow throws,
Where no cooling water flows,
Where the hot air is not stirred
By the wing of singing bird,
There thou goest, untired and meek,
Day by day, and week by week,
With thy load of precious things—
Silks for merchants, gold for kings,

Pearls of Ormuz, riches rare,
Damascene and Indian ware
Bale on bale, and heap on heap—
Freighted like a costly ship!
And when week by week is gone,
And the traveller journeys on
Feebly; when his strength is fled,
And his hope and heart seem dead,
Camel, thou dost turn thine eye
On him kindly, soothingly,
As if thou wouldst. cheering, say,
"Journey on for this one day—
Do not let thy heart despond!
There is water yet beyond!
I can scent it in the air—
Do not let thy heart despair!"
And thou guid'st the traveller there.

Camel, thou art good and mild,
Docile as a little child;
Thou wast made for usefulness,
Man to comfort and to bless;
And the desert wastes would be
Untrack'd regions but for thee!

Mary Howitt.

THE POLAR BEAR.

Ex-is'-tence	His-tor'-i-cal	Un-for'-tu-nate
E-ter'-nal	E-nor'-mous	Ad-van'-tage
Ear'-li-er	Ac-com'-mo-da-ting	Car'case
Arc'-tic	Ap-proach'-es	Vic-to'-ri-ous
Voy'-a-gers	Stealth'-i-ly	Ap'-pe-tite
Op-po'-nent	Ban'-quet	Un-fre'-quent-ly

There is a kind of bear which passes its existence either in the water, or on the ice, or on land. This is the white polar bear, whose dwelling is found among the eternal frosts of the North Pole. It is a large and powerful animal, although not quite so large or so powerful as represented by some of the earlier Arctic voyagers, one of whom tells us that he and his comrades killed a bear whose skin was twenty-three feet in length. Another relates that bears frequently carried off seamen and devoured them within sight of their friends, who were unable to prevent their capture, or to release them afterwards. Yet it is a dangerous opponent, and does not yield its life without a severe struggle.

The polar bear is almost an historical animal, as Nelson once nearly lost his life in an attempt to kill one with an unloaded musket, foolishly imagining that he could knock down the animal with the gun stock. Indeed, had it not been for a wide rift in the ice, England would have lost a youth who afterwards became one of her greatest heroes. Who could have thought at the time that such weighty consequences lay between a blow of a musket, and a stroke from a bear's paw?

The colour of the polar bear is a yellowish white; the fur is short and fine over the back, but lengthens considerably towards the under part of the body. The feet are particularly bushy, and are also furnished with a plentiful supply of fur on the under surfaces, in order to give the animal a firmer hold on the ice.

The swimming powers of this animal are very great, and, indeed, are required in its chase of fish and seals. The latter animal is, however, so good a swimmer itself, that the bear does not care to chase it in the water, but generally contrives to surprise it when asleep on a piece of ice. When chasing a seal in this position, the bear approaches very stealthily, making long dives, and so managing that at his last dive he comes up directly under the unfortunate seal. He either tumbles into the water in a fright, and is instantly snapped up, or is chased on the ice, where the bear has the advantage in point of speed, and is sure to catch him. But the great banquet of the bear is upon a dead whale, on which in company with sharks, sea birds, &c., he feeds, until the carcase is so stripped that the weight of the bones sinks it, and the sharks have it all to themselves.

But the prey which gives the most trouble is the walrus. This enormous seal is often attacked by the bears, but fights with such fury, that it not unfrequently comes off victorious in the struggle. Many a walrus has been killed, bearing on its body scars, the results of battles with the polar bears. In the absence of large prey, such as whales and seals, the white bear does not disdain fish, sea birds and their eggs, and, with an accommodating appetite, often feeds on roots and berries.

Wood's Nat. Hist.

SAM, THE PET DOG.

Re-triev'-er	Laugh'-a-ble	Host'-ler
Ken'-nel	Cel'-e-bra-ted	O-be'-di-ence
Ex'-er-cis-ing	In-vit'-ed	Mod'-el

A dark brown retriever, named Sam, was in the habit of going into a kennel of hounds, who always crowded round and caressed him. When they were in the field exercising, Sam was told to go and amuse them, he then went among them, jumped, and played all sorts of antics. leaping and tumbling about in the most laughable manner,—they looking amused at him the while.

He went with his master to call upon a lady; she patted him, asked if he were the celebrated Sam, and, hearing he was, she invited him to stay with her. Sam's owner petted and praised him; told him to be a good dog, and to stay with the lady, until she had given him his breakfast on the following morning. The dog was contented to remain; ate his breakfast in the morning;

then, looking up in the lady's face, wagged his tail, left the house, and ran home.

He was in the habit of fetching his master's clothes, and of returning them to their proper places; and he knew their names. He sat in a chair at dinner with the family without making any confusion; or dined alone, alternately taking a piece of bread and meat, and then drinking a little milk; and if any one said, "Give me a piece, Sam?" he instantly obeyed.

When all was gone, he cleared away the things. He would fetch his master's horse from the inn, pay the hostler, and ride back upon the saddle. In short, he seemed to understand every thing that was said to him, and he was a model of good nature and obedience.

Mrs. Lee.

A PRICELESS DOG.

Pas'-sen-gers	Coun'-te-nance	Pre-serv'-er
De-vo'-tion	At-tract'-ed	Ex-pres'-sion
Con-fu'-sion	Ex-cite'-ment	Ca-nal'
Has'-ti-ly	An-nounced'	In-tense'

A gentleman was lately returning from a visit to New Orleans, in a steamer, with but a few passengers. Among the ladies, one especially interested him. She was the wife of a wealthy planter, returning with an only child to her father's house ; and her devotion to this child was touching.

While passing through the canal of Louisville, the steamer stopped for a few moments at the quay. The nurse, wishing to see the city, was stepping ashore when the child suddenly sprang from her arms into the terrible current that swept towards the falls, and disappeared immediately. The confusion which ensued attracted the attention of a gentleman who was sitting in the fore part of the boat, quietly reading. Rising hastily, he asked for some article the child had worn. The nurse handed him a tiny apron she had torn off in her efforts to save the child as it fell. Turning to a splendid Newfoundland dog that was eagerly watching his countenance, the gentleman pointed first to the apron, and then to the spot where the child had sunk.

In an instant, the noble dog leapt into the water, and disappeared. By this time the excitement was intense, and some person on shore supposing that the dog was lost, as well as the child, procured a boat and started to search for the body.

Just at this moment the dog was seen far away with something in his mouth. Bravely he struggled with the waves, but it was clear his strength was failing fast, and more than one breast gave a sigh of relief as the boat reached him and it was announced that he was still alive. They were brought on board—the dog and the child.

Giving a single glance to satisfy herself that the child was really living, the young mother rushed forward, and sinking beside the dog, threw her arm around his neck and burst into tears. Not many could bear the sight unmoved, and as she caressed and kissed his shaggy head, she looked up to his owner and said :—

"Oh, sir, I must have this dog, take all I have—everything—but give me my child's preserver."

The gentleman smiled, and patting his dog's head, said, "I am very glad, madam, he has been of service to you, but nothing in the world could induce me to part with him."

The dog looked as though he perfectly understood what they were talking about, and giving his sides a shake, laid himself down at his master's feet, with an expression in his large eyes that said plainer than words, "No! nothing shall part us."

Anon.

AN INGENIOUS DOG.

Pau′-pers	Ex-hib′-its	In-ge-nu′-i-ty
Char′-i-ta-ble	Por′-tions	Vict′-uals
Pen′-sion-er	Sus-pi′-cions	Con′-stant-ly
Re-lig′-ious	Pa′-tience	Ma-chine′

At a convent in France twenty paupers were served with a dinner at a certain hour every day. A dog belonging to the convent did not fail to be present at this meal, to receive the scraps which were now and then thrown to him. The paupers, however, were hungry, and, of course, not very charitable, so that their pensioner did little more than scent the feast of what he would fain have partaken.

The portions were served by a person at the ringing of a bell, and delivered out by means of what in religious houses is called a *tour*. This is a machine like the half of a basin, that, on being turned round, exhibits whatever has been placed in it, without discovering the person at the other side who moves it.

One day this dog, which had received only a few scraps, waited till all the paupers had left; he then took the rope in his mouth and rung the bell. The trick succeeded. He repeated it the next day, with the same good fortune. At length the cook finding that twenty-one portions were given out instead of twenty, was determined to discover the thief. He accordingly lay in wait for him, and his suspicions at last fell on the dog. This proved to be a fact, on his seeing the animal remain with great patience till the paupers had all gone, and then pull the bell.

The story was told to the monks; and to reward him for his ingenuity the dog was allowed to ring the bell everyday, and a mess of broken victuals was henceforth constantly served out to him.

Bingley.

THE STORMY PETREL.

A thousand miles from land are we,
Tossing about on the roaring sea,
From billow to bounding billow cast,
Like fleecy snow on the stormy blast;
The sails are scatter'd about like weeds,
The strong masts shake like quivering reeds;
The mighty cables and iron chains,
The hull which all earthly strength disdains,
They strain and they crack; and hearts of stone
Their natural, hard, proud strength disown.

Up and down! up and down!
From the base of the wave to the billow's crown,
Amidst the flashing and feathery foam,
The stormy petrel finds a home;
A home—if such a place can be
For her who lives on the wide, wide sea,
On the craggy ice, in the frozen air,
And only seeking her rocky lair
To warn her young, and teach them to spring,
At once o'er the waves on their stormy wing!

O'er the deep! o'er the deep!
Where the whale, and the shark, and the swordfish sleep,
Outflying the blast and the driving rain,
The petrel telleth her tale in vain:
For the mariner curseth the warning bird,
Who bringeth him news of the storm unheard:
Ah! thus does the prophet of good or ill
Meet hate from the creatures he serveth still;
Yet, he never falters,—so, petrel, spring
Once more o'er the waves on thy stormy wing.

Barry Cornwall.

THE SWALLOW.

-tu-al′-i-ty	Toil′-some	Won′-drous-ly
u-lar′-i-ty	Re-cord′-ed	Prov′-i-dence
n′-tions	Gra′-cious-ly	Pres′-ence
t′-ed	Ar-range′-ment	Vent′-ures
-mist	Cher′-ish	Tur′-tle

nong the signs which tell us that winter has passed , and that spring has come, we see with gladness raceful flight of the swallow; and so regularly does pear, that no traveller from a distant country ever rmed his journey with such punctuality. That bird and his companions have come to us from a. They have crossed the sea and the land, and on their course, not only to the same countries, ven to the same houses which gave them shelter in a er year. And this they have done without map or ass, yet with a speed and regularity which surpass at our boasted human inventions could attempt. may we say with the sacred writer, "The stork e heaven knoweth her appointed times; and the , and the crane, and the swallow observe the time eir coming."

d now, having come, they set about the great ess which they have to do—namely, the building eir nests and the rearing of their young. The ent kinds take different situations, and build in ent ways. The sand-martin hollows out his dwell- n the face of a sand-bank; the house-martin fixes est under the eaves of our houses, or in the corners e windows. The swallow builds in the shaft of an d chimney; and frequently in the space between eams and the rafters of an out-house. He does however, confine himself to the outside of houses; entures at times into the dwellings of man, and even into places where we should least expect to see him. Thus, a few years ago, a pair of swallows built their nest in a school-room in the county of Antrim, in Ireland, and carried on their labours during the hours of school—a window having been left open to allow them to fly in and out. The boys, I am glad to say, never disturbed or injured the birds. The fact of the swallow coming in our own day into the dwellings, and frequently into the houses of worship erected by man, is similar to that recorded by the Psalmist nearly three thousand years ago—"The sparrow hath an house, and the swallow a nest for herself, where she may lay her young—even Thine altars, O Lord of Hosts, my king and my God."

During the time the house-martin and the swallow are building their nests, it is a pleasant thing to watch their movements—to see them coming home with the mud, the straw, or the feather, which the nest at that time requires, and then in a moment starting off to seek for more. How busy they are! How busy, yet how happy! They are fulfilling their appointed task. To them labour is not toilsome. We cannot doubt that God has been graciously pleased to make it a source of high enjoyment. Their work goes on for fourteen or sixteen hours out of the twenty-four; yet next morning they begin it again, as brisk as ever, long before man has risen from his bed, and entered on the duties of another day.

The eggs are laid, the young are hatched, and now they must be fed. Early and late the parents are seeking to supply their wants. Ever on the wing, chasing and catching the quick-moviug insects, and dashing through the clouds of flies that are seen above the tops of trees or over pools of water. Wherever the insects are, there are the swallows. In fine weather insects keep high in the air; but when they feel a change of weather is nigh, they fly lower. When swallows are flying high, we say there is going to be fine weather; but when they skim near the ground or the surface of the pools, we say rain is coming. They are busy about their prey, they are intent on that object alone, and yet the manner in which they fly warns us of a coming change.

Let us think a little on their long continued flight. A horse or a dog would be wearied in half the time that they are daily on the wing. Yet they do what seems a more difficult thing than running along the ground. They support themselves in the air, though their bodies are much heavier than air; and they not only do so, but move at a rate which leaves the quickest of our railway trains far behind. How is this done? It is done by means of the beautiful arrangement of the several parts of their bodies. The framework is strong and yet not heavy. The bones are light, and are also hollow. The air they breathe goes into the bones, and through every part of their bodies, entering even into the feathers. The extent of wing, the strength of muscle, and the shape of the body, are all adapted for movement in the air, and give to such birds the power of rapid and long-continued flight.

Let us cherish them about our dwellings, protect them from injury, seek not to disturb them or their young, but look upon both as creatures wondrously framed by Him to whom we ourselves are indebted for life, and for all the blessings with which it is accompanied. And, if He in His good providence should permit us to live until the swallow again returns, may we hail it with still kindlier feelings, as a creature acting under the guidance of an unseen hand.

Such thoughts will add to the pleasure with which we look upon this graceful bird, and increase our enjoyment of the scenes which are gladdened by the presence of this " guest of summer."

"Oh! what a host of joyous thoughts arise,
When first we mark the swallow's restless wing;
What dreams of sunny days, of twilight skies,
Of flowers that wait the breath of June to spring."

Robert Patterson.

THE ELEPHANT.

Jui'-cy	E-nough'	Six'-pence
Ex-am'-ple	Urged	Mis'-er-y
Cra'-dle	Ef'-fort	El'-e-phant

An elephant is first in size, and in sense, of all the beasts of the field, and when used kindly he puts forth great strength, and works hard to help and serve his master. The trunk of the elephant is of more use to him than our hands are to us. With it he takes up food and water, and puts them into his mouth. This trunk will pick up a sixpence, and lift a heavy load; tear down trees, and undo locks and bolts of doors.

The elephant smells by means of his trunk, and breathes through it. He feeds upon the tall juicy grass of India, and digs up roots, and can reach the young sprays, and pull down the ripe fruits of the palm and other trees.

In India he helps to build ships. Long planks of wood, that twenty men could not move, are drawn along quite easily by him. Round a heavy beam, for example, a strong rope is tied, the end of which one takes up, and twists it round his trunk. He has the sense to draw it between, or raise it over things lying in the way to the ship-side.

A poor woman who had been kind to an elephant

often left her child in his care while she went out to work. When the woman died he would not let the child go out of his sight, and would not eat until it was laid in its cradle at his feet. When the child was old enough to crawl about, he gently held it back with the trunk from harm, just as a kind nurse would guard her little charge.

In war-time elephants are used to drag the heavy guns and cannon—often up a steep hill-side. When driven back after a battle, they never tread on the wounded men, but lift them with care, and lay them aside, and so make room to pass. Even at a rapid pace they can do this, and that with the greatest care.

An elephant was bid drag a great load up a steep and bad road. He tried, and did his best; then stopped short, as if to show that it could not be done. The owner said in a harsh voice, "Take that lazy beast away, and bring a better one." The poor creature knew what the unjust words meant, and made one last effort, which moved the load, but cost the life of the elephant: it fell down dead on the spot.

Some elephants had to pass over a bridge, and their sense enabled them to know that it was not safe. The first would not set a foot on the bridge, and when pricked to go on, it turned back in a rage, and no one could stop it. The next stood still at the foot of the bridge. It was pricked and urged on for a time, in vain. At last, with a deep groan, it went on. Before it got to the middle the bridge fell with a crash, and the elephant was thrown upon the sharp rough rocks below.

The last elephant saw it all, and made its way down a steep bank, to reach its friend before death put an end to pain and misery.

Book of Beasts.

THE SQUIRREL.

I'm a merry, merry squirrel,
All day I leap and whirl
Through my home in the old beech-tree;
If you chase me, I will run,
In the shade and in the sun,
But you never, never can catch me!
For round a bough I'll creep,
Playing hide-and-seek so sly,
Or through the leaves bo-peep,
With my little shining eye.

Up and down I run and frisk,
With my bushy tail to whisk
All who mope in the old beech-trees;
How droll to see the owl
As I make him wink and growl,
When his sleepy, sleepy head I tease!
And I waken up the bat,
Who flies off with a scream,
For he thinks that I'm the cat
Pouncing on him in his dream.

Through all the summer long
I never want a song,
From my birds in the old beech-trees;
I have singers all the night,
And with the morning bright,
Come my busy humming fat brown bees.
When I 've nothing else to do,
With the nursing birds I sit,
And we laugh at the cuckoo
A-cuckooing to her tit.

When winter comes with snow,
And its cruel tempests blow
All the leaves from my old beech-trees,
Then beside the wren and mouse
I furnish up a house,
Where like a prince I live at my ease!
What care I for hail or sleet,
With my cosy cap and coat;
And my tail upon my feet,
Or wrapped about my throat!

Good Words.

THE LION AND THE SPANIEL.

Ad-mis′-sion	Cu-ri-os′-i-ty	Pro-tec′-tor
Nov′-el-ty	Ac-quaint′-ance	Des′-o-late
Do-min′-ions	Ap′-pe-tite	Ex-haust′-ed
De-sir′-ous	Ten′-der-ness	Grad′-u-al-ly
Cus′-tom-a-ry	Pa′-tron	Ac-cept′-ing
Span′-iel	Ad-ver-tised′	Plen′-ti-ful-ly

In the afternoon our company went to the Tower, to satisfy ourselves as to the truth of the wonderful story of the great lion and the little dog.

We found the place thronged, and all were obliged to pay high prices of admission, on account of the novelty of the show; so that the keeper, in a short time, made a little fortune.

The great cage in front was occupied by a beast, who was called the king's lion; and, while he traversed the limits of his straitened dominions, he was attended by a small and very beautiful black spaniel, who frisked and gambolled about him. At one time it would pretend to snarl and bite at the lion; at another, the noble animal, with an air of fondness, would hold down his head, while the tiny creature licked his terrible chaps. Their history, as the keeper related, was this :—

It was customary for all, who were unable or unwilling to pay their sixpence, to bring a dog or cat as an offering to the beast in place of money to the keeper. Among others, a fellow had caught up this pretty black spaniel in the streets, and it was thrown into the cage of the great lion. Immediately the little animal trembled and shivered with fear, and threw itself on its back. It then put forth its tongue, and held up its paws, as if praying for mercy.

In the meantime, the lordly brute, instead of devouring it, beheld it with an eye of cool curiosity. He turned it over with one paw, and then with the other; sniffed at it, and seemed desirous of courting a further acquaintance.

The keeper, on seeing this, brought a large mess of his own family dinner; but the lion kept aloof, and refused to eat, keeping his eye on the dog, and, as it were inviting it to eat. At length the little animal's fears being somewhat abated, and its appetite being quickened by the smell of the victuals, it approached slowly, and tremblingly ventured to eat. The lion then advanced gently and began to partake, and they finished their meal very lovingly together.

From this day the strictest friendship commenced between them, a friendship consisting of all possible affection and tenderness on the part of the lion, and of the utmost confidence and boldness on the part of the dog; insomuch that he would lay himself down to sleep within the fangs and under the jaws of his terrible patron.

A gentleman who had lost the spaniel, and had advertised a reward of two guineas to the finder, at length heard of the adventure, and went to claim his dog. "You see, sir," said the keeper, "it would be a great pity to part such loving friends; however, if you insist upon your property being restored, you must even be pleased to take him yourself: it is a task that I would not engage in for five hundred guineas." The gentleman of course declined the risk of a dispute with the lion.

In about twelve months the little spaniel sickened and died, and left its loving protector the most desolate of creatures. For a time the lion did not appear to believe otherwise than that his pet was asleep. He would continue to smell the body; then would stir it with his nose, and turn it over with his paws. But finding that all his efforts to awake his pet were vain, he would traverse his cage from end to end at a swift and uneasy pace, then stop, and look down with a fixed and drooping gaze; then raise his head, and open his horrible throat, and utter a prolonged roar, as of distant thunder, for minutes together.

They attempted, but in vain, to take away the carcase from him ; he watched it constantly, and would suffer no one to touch it. The keeper then endeavoured to tempt him with a variety of food, but he turned from all that was offered with loathing. They then put several living dogs into his cage, and these he instantly tore piecemeal, but left their bodies, untasted, on the floor.

His passion being thus inflamed, he would dart his fangs into the boards and wrench away large splinters ; and again grapple at the bars of his cage, and seem enraged at his restraint. Again, quite exhausted, he would stretch himself by the remains of his friend, gather them in with his paws, and hug them. The while he uttered under-roars of terrible melancholy for the loss of his little play-fellow—the only friend, the only companion that he had upon earth.

For five days he thus languished, and gradually declined, without taking any food or accepting any comfort. At last, one morning, he was found dead, with his head lovingly reclined on the carcase of his little friend.

They were both buried together, and their grave was plentifully watered by the tears of the keeper and his loudly lamenting family.

Brooke.

A WASP THE FIRST PAPER MAKER.

Ad-van'-tage	Ex'-cel-lent	Bus'-iness
Fi'-bre	Pa'-per-mak-ers	Coarse
Ex-am'-ine	Be-gin'-ning	Knowl'-edge
Ex-act'-ly	In-stinct'-ive	Per'-fect
Ma-te'-ri-al	Far'-ther	Su-pe'-ri-or

"Here is a part of a wasp's nest, which we have found," said some children to their father; "and as you told us it was always best to notice everything closely, we examined this, and it appeared so much like coarse paper, that we thought man did not make the first paper in the world."

"Well, children, that was not a bad thought. Now you see the advantage of taking notice of things, and of thinking about what you see. You are perfectly right in supposing that wasps make paper; but it was a long time before men found out what they made it of.

"A gentleman was trying for twenty years, he says, to find out how the wasp made paper, before he succeeded. At last he one day saw a female wasp alight on the sash of his window, and begin to gnaw the wood; he watched her, and saw that she pulled off from the wood fibre after fibre, about the tenth part of an inch long, and not so large as a hair. She gathered these into a knot with her feet, and then flew away to another part of the sash, and went again to work stripping off more fibres or threads, and adding them to the bundle she had already had. At last he caught her in order to amine the bundle, and found that its colour was actly like that of a wasp's nest.

" He then set to work himself with his penknife, and ry soon scraped and bruised some of the wood of the ne window sash, so as to make a ball exactly like the sp's. He thought this was the material out of which wasp made paper; and it has since been proved that was right.

" The animal wets her little bundle of bruised wooden res or threads with a kind of glue that she has, and s makes it stick together like pulp or paste; and ile it is soft, the wasp walks backwards and forwards, d spreads it out with her feet and tongue, until she s made it almost as thin as the thinnest paper. rnets make paper for their nests much in the same nner as the wasps do, only it is coarser."

" Well, then, we were right in thinking that wasps re the first papermakers; and very glad we are that saw this old piece of a wasp's nest. Who would ve thought that so much could be learned by picking this old scrap ?"

" Very good sense, children, in that thought. A wise n will learn something from almost anything. Use ur eyes, and think of what you see. This very trade papermaking, I think man would have found out a od deal sooner, if he had watched the wasps at their rk. They have been excellent workmen at this siness from the beginning; and man has gone on rning little by little of this very trade, when he might ve made a long step at once, had he but noticed wasps d hornets.

" We go on very slowly sometimes, in learning to ke a trade as perfect as it can be, while the poor imal, with the instinctive knowledge which God gave is often our superior. These dumb animals cannot ch us everything; there is a point to which they can go, and no farther; but as far as they do know, their knowledge is perfect; and I have no doubt that a great many useful things, not now known, will hereafter be found out by watching the lower animals."

Constable's Series.

THE UNFORTUNATE SPIDER.

In a little dark crack, half a yard from the ground,
  An honest old spider resided:
So pleasant, and snug, and convenient 'twas found,
That his friends came to see it from many miles round;
  It seemed for his pleasure provided.

Of the cares and fatigues, and distresses of life,
  This spider was thoroughly tired;
So, leaving those scenes of contention and strife,
His children all settled, he came with his wife
  To live in this cranny retired.

He thought that the little his wife would consume
  'Twould be easy for him to provide her,
Forgetting he lived in a gentleman's house
Where came every morning a maid and a broom,
  Those pitiless foes to a spider.

For when (as sometimes it would chance to befall)
  Just when his neat web was completed,
Brush came the great broom down the side of the wall,
And perhaps carried with it web, spider, and all,
  He thought himself cruelly treated.

One day, when their cupboard was empty and dry,
  His wife (Mrs. Hairy-leg-spinner)
Said to him "Dear, go to the cobweb and try,
If you can't find the leg or the wing of fly,
  As a bit of a relish for dinner."

Directly he went, his long search to resume,
  For nothing he ever denied her,
Alas ! little guessing his terrible doom;
Just then came the gentleman into his room,
  And saw the unfortunate spider.

So, while the poor fellow, in search of his pelf,
  In the cobweb continued to linger,
The gentleman reached a long cane from the shelf,
For certain good reasons best known to himself
  Preferring his stick to his finger.

Then presently poking him down to the floor,
  Not stopping at all to consider,
With one horrid crush the whole business was o'er,
The poor little spider was heard of no more,
  To the lasting distress of his widow.

Taylor.

THE WILD CAT.

In-hab'-its	Kit'-tens	Re-cov'-er-y
Moun'-tain-ous	Mew'-ing	Ter'-ror
Hav'-oc	Crash'-ing	Un-earth'-ly
Fol'-low-ing	Brist'-ling	Fu'-ri-ous
An'-ec-dote	Piv'-ot	De-struc'-tive

The wild cat inhabits the woods of mountainous countries. He lives on birds, rabbits, hares, rats, and mice; and creates havoc amongst poultry, lambs, kids, fawns, &c. He is much larger than the common cat. Some have been caught in America which measured, from the nose to the end of the tail, upwards of five feet. His hair is soft and fine; of a pale yellowish colour, mixed with grey; his tail is thick and long; and he is one of the fiercest and most destructive beasts of prey.

A traveller in one of the western states of America relates the following anecdote of one : —

"I was plodding on in a waggon, over a level road in the hot noon sun of a June day. Some ten yards ahead of me, a wild cat, leading three kittens, came out of the wood, crossed the road, and went into the bushes on my left. I thought what nice pets they would make, and wished I had one.

"When I came up I noticed one of the young ones at the edge of the bushes but a few feet off, and I heard, or thought I heard, the old one stealing along deep in the woods. I sprang out, snatched up the kitten, threw it into the waggon, jumped in, and started. When I laid hands on it, it mewed and kept mewing, and as I grasped the reins I heard a sharp growl and a crashing through the bush.

"I knew the old one was coming, and the next instant she sprang over the hedge and alighted in the road. She ran with her eyes flaming, her hair bristling, and her teeth grinning. She turned as on a pivot, and gave an unearthly squall, as she saw me driving away. Then, bounding after me with furious yells, she gained on me so fast that from very fear, I threw the kitten out and lashed the flying horse. The enraged animal halted for a moment to see that her kitten was safe; and then continued the chase, as though the recovery of her young one would not suffice without revenge.

"When I saw her at my back, I scarcely breathed for terror. At last her crying child recalled her. At this point I ventured to look back, and saw her standing with her young one in her mouth looking after me, as though she had half a mind to drop the kitten and give chase again. Urging on my horse, I did not feel quite safe until I had got some miles away. I made up my mind from that time forward to let kittens alone and mind my own business."

Anon.

THE MAN AND THE SNAKE.

Once on a time, as Æsop tells,
  A man in winter's iron weather,
Found on the bare and wind-swept fells,
  A snake, its coils frost-bound together.

He raised the creature from the ground,
  And was about to fling it by,
When lo! some spark of life he found
  Still glowing in its evil eye.

The man whose large compassion ranged
  E'en to that reptile most unblest,
Sudden his idle purpose changed,
  And placed the serpent in his breast.

Under his kindly bosom's glow,
  Slowly the stiffened coils outdrew;
The thickening blood resumed its flow,
  The snaky instincts waked anew.

The man was glad to feel awake,
  The crawling life within his vest;
For to have harboured even a snake,
  Is pleasure in a gen'rous breast.

Sudden he stops, with shriek and start—
  Then falls a corpse, all swollen and black!
The snake's fell tooth had pierced the heart,
  Whose warmth to life had brought it back.

Punch.

——o——

THE FISH AND THEIR LITTLE MISTRESS.

Hith'-er-to	Un-tam'-a-ble	Pre'-vi-ous
Re-sid'-ing	De-grees'	Daugh'-ter
Mis-tak'-en	Mis'-tress	Ev'-i-dent
Dis-ap-point'-ment	Clus'-ter-ing	Tor'-toise

There was once a little girl six years old, residing in America, who had a most wonderful control over a class of animals hitherto thought to be untamable.

For a year or two previous, the little girl was in the habit of playing about the pond near her dwelling, and throwing crumbs into the water for the fish. By degrees these timid creatures became so tame as to come at her call, follow her about the pond, and eat from her hand.

A gentleman went down there with his daughter, to see the little creatures and their mistress. At first the fish were mistaken, and came up to the top of the water as the strangers approached; but in a moment they discovered their mistake, and whisked away in evident disappointment. Their own mistress then came up and called, and they crowded towards her, clustering about her hands to receive the crumbs.

She had, besides, a turtle, or tortoise, which had been injured in one of its feet. This creature lived in the pond, and seemed to be entirely under the control of the little girl, obeying her voice, and feeding from her hand.

It was charming to see the bright-eyed girl sporting with her obedient swarms of the finny tribe, touching their sides, and letting them slip through her hands

Anon.

—o—

SECTION IV.

WHO IS THIS, AND WHAT IS HIS NAME?

Eight'-een	Mar'-vel-lous	Blas-phem'-er
Ap-pear'-ance	As-ton'-ished	Con-demn'-ed
An-nounced'	Bur'-i-al	Tri'-umph
Man'-ger	En'-e-mies	Hymns
Coun'-try-men	Jeal'-ous	In'-ter-est
Proph'-et	Gov'-ern-or	Vis'-ions

Eighteen hundred years ago, there appeared in the East a child such as the world has never seen either before or since. In outward form and appearance he was like other children; but in his soul within he was pure as angel in heaven. He was born in a stable; but his birth was announced by angels, and a star guided a company of wise men to the manger which was his cradle.

When about thirty years of age, he went forth among his countrymen, to teach them the way to be good and happy. He led so holy a life, that wicked men stood in awe, and were afraid of him; he taught so many holy and heavenly things, that good men said he was a prophet; and the works he did were so marvellous, that all men were astonished at them. He had power to heal all manner of sickness and disease. He often gave sight to the blind, and hearing to the deaf, and speech to the dumb. He could calm the stormy sea and the raging wind by merely saying "Peace, be still!" And three several times did he bring back to life those who were dead;—once, in the case of a maiden newly dead; again, in the case of a youth, the only son of a widow, whom his friends were carrying to his burial; and yet again, in the case of a man who had lain three days in the grave. This mighty power, too, he never used except for the purpose of doing good. He refused to call down fire from heaven to destroy wicked men, though urged by some of his friends to do so. But never did he refuse to perform an act of kindness. He went about doing good.

Yet though thus good and kind, he had many enemies, who hated him, and evil-entreated him. Some of the chief men of the country were jealous of him; some were afraid of him; others said he was mad; and all joined together to plot his death. And at last these wicked men prevailed. They seized him by force, and dragged him before the governor, pretending that he was a blasphemer, and a stirrer up of the people. And this unjust governor, to please these wicked men, condemned him to die, and had him put to the bitter and shameful death of the cross.

But the triumph of his enemies was short. Before he had lain three days in the tomb, he rose again from the dead, and showed himself alive to many. And at the end of forty days, whilst he was in the act of lifting up his hands and blessing his friends, he was parted from them, and carried up into heaven. Since then he has never been seen on earth, except by some good men in dreams and visions. But it is certain that he still lives in heaven, and takes an interest in the things done here on earth. From age to age, too, his friends have been evermore increasing; so that they are now a multitude which no man can number. They love him, though they see him not; they pray to him, and sing hymns to him; they set apart every week a day to his honour; they count it their chief glory to walk in his eps, and suffer for his sake: and they look onward ith joyful hope to the time when he shall return from eaven with power and great glory, to put his enemies everlasting shame, and to take themselves to dwell ith him in eternal glory.

Who is this, and what is his name?

M'Culloch's Series.

FAITH.

We saw Thee not, when Thou didst tread,
O Saviour, this our sinful earth;
Nor heard Thy voice restore the dead,
And wake them to a second birth:
But we *believe* that Thou didst come,
And quit for us Thy glorious home.

We were not with the faithful few,
Who stood Thy bitter cross around,—
Nor heard Thy prayer for those who slew,
Nor felt the earthquake rock the ground,—
We saw no spear-wound pierce Thy side:
Yet we *believe* that Thou hast died.

No angel's message met our ear,
On that first glorious Easter-day,—
"The Lord is risen, He is not here,
Come see the place where Jesus lay!"
But we *believe* that Thou didst quell
The banded powers of Death and Hell.

We saw Thee not return on high;
And now our longing sight to bless,
No ray of glory from the sky
Comes down upon our wilderness:
Yet we *believe* that Thou art there,
And seek Thee, Lord, in praise and prayer.

Rugby Hymn Book.

TRAVELLERS' WONDERS.

Quad'-ru-ped	De-li'-cious	Ti'-ni-est
Trans-pa'-rent	Tem'-per-a-ture	For'-eign-er
Pow'-dered	Nour'-ish-ment	Cat'-er-pil-lar
Un-pal'-a-ta-ble	Pe-cul'-iar	Un-in-tel'-li-gi-ble
Ad-di'-tion	Dis-guis'-ing	Man-u-fac'-tured
Nau'-seous	For'-mi-da-ble	Sa-lut'-ing

One winter evening, as Captain Compass was sitting by the fire, with his children all around him, he began, after being coaxed a little, to tell them the following story : —

I was once, at this time of the year, in a country where it was very cold, and the poor inhabitants had much ado to keep themselves from starving. They were clad partly in the skins of animals, and partly in garments made from the outer covering of a middle-sized quadruped, which they were so cruel as to cut off his back while he was alive.

They dwelt in dwellings, part of which was sunk under ground. The materials were either stones, or earth hardened by fire; and so violent in that country were the storms of wind and rain, that many of them covered their roofs all over with stones. The walls of their houses had holes to let in the light; but to prevent the cold air and wet from coming in, they were covered with a sort of transparent stone, made of melted sand or flints. As wood was rather scarce, I know not what they would have done for firing, had they not discovered in the bowels of the earth a very extraordinary kind of stone, which when put among burning wood, caught fire and flamed like a torch.

Well—but their diet too was remarkable. Some of them ate fish that had been hung up in smoke till they were quite dry and hard; and along with it they ate either the roots of plants, or a sort of coarse black cake made of powdered seeds. These were the poorer class : the richer had a whiter kind of cake, which they were fond of daubing over with a greasy matter; this was the product of a certain large animal. This grease they used, too, in almost all their dishes, and when fresh, it really was not unpalatable. They likewise devoured the flesh of many birds and beasts when they could get it; and ate the leaves and other parts of a variety of vegetables growing in the country, some absolutely raw, others variously prepared by the aid of fire.

Another great article of food was the curd of milk, pressed into a hard mass and salted. This had so rank a smell, that persons of weak stomachs often could not bear to come near it. For drink, they made great use of water in which certain dry leaves had been steeped. These leaves I was told, came from a great distance. They had likewise a method of preparing a liquor of the seeds of a grass-like plant steeped in water, with the addition of a bitter herb, and then set to "work" or *ferment*. I was prevailed upon to taste it, and thought it at first nauseous enough, but in time I liked it pretty well.

When I had sojourned in this cold climate about half a year, I found the same people enjoying a delicious temperature and a country full of beauty and verdure. The trees and shrubs were furnished with a great variety of fruits, which with other vegetable products, made up a large part of the food of the inhabitants. I particularly relished certain berries growing in bunches, some white and some red, of a very pleasant sourish taste, and so transparent, that one might see the seeds at their very centre. Here were whole fields full of extremely sweet-smelling flowers, which they told me were succeeded by pods bearing seeds, that afforded good nourishment to man and beast. A great variety of birds enlivened the groves and woods; among which I was entertained with one, that, with little teaching, spoke as plainly as a parrot.

The people were tolerably gentle and civilized, and possessed many of the arts of life. Their dress in warm weather was very various. Many were clad only in a thin cloth made of the long fibres of the stalk of a plant cultivated for the purpose: this they prepared by soaking in water, and then beating with large mallets. Others wore cloth woven from a sort of vegetable wool, growing in pods upon bushes. But the most singular material was a fine glossy stuff, used chiefly by the richer classes, which, as I was credibly informed, is manufactured out of the webs of a certain kind of grub-worm. This is a most wonderful circumstance, if we consider the immense number necessary to the production of so large a quantity of the stuff as I saw used.

This people are very peculiar in their dress, especially the women: their clothing consists of a great number of articles impossible to be described, and strangely disguising the natural form of the body. In some instances they seem very cleanly; but in others, the Hottentots can scarcely go beyond them. Their mode of dressing the hair is remarkable: it is all matted and stiffened with the fat of swine and other animals, mixed up with powders of various kinds and colours. Like many Indian nations, they use feathers in the head-dress. One thing surprised me much, which was, that they bring up in their houses an animal of the tiger kind, with formidable teeth and claws, which is played with and caressed by the tiniest and most timid of their children.

"I am sure I would not play with it," said Jack.

"Why, you might chance to get an ugly scratch if you did," said the Captain.

The language of this nation seems very harsh and unintelligible to a foreigner, yet they talk to one another with great ease and quickness. One of the oddest customs is that which men use on saluting each other. Let the weather be what it will, they uncover their heads, and remain uncovered for some time, if they mean to be extremely respectful.

"Why, that's like pulling off our hats," said Jack. "Ah, ha! Papa," cried Betsy, "I have found you out. You have been telling us of our own country and what is done at home all this while." "But," said Jack, "we don't burn stones, nor eat grease and powdered seeds, nor wear skins and webs, nor play with tigers." "No?" said the captain; "pray what are coals but stones; and is not butter, grease; and corn, seeds; and leather, skins; and silk the web of a kind of caterpillar; and may we not as well call a cat an animal of the tiger kind, as a tiger an animal of the cat kind?"

Evenings at Home.

CLEVER BOYS.

Clev'-er-ness	Hon'-est-ly	De-fi'-cient
Rec-om-mend'	Per-se-ver'-ing	Qual'-i-ties
Prin'-ci-ple	Un-prof'-i-ta-ble	Quest'-ions
Ne-ces'-si-ty	Use'-ful-ness	A-bil'-i-ty

Do not talk to me about a boy being clever, for if he have nothing but cleverness to recommend him, I think but little better of him than if you told me he could dance the sailor's hornpipe.

The broad sails of a gay-rigged ship are pleasant to gaze on, but if the vessel have no ballast, those broad sails may be the means of her destruction. In like manner, the cleverness of a boy may attract attention, but if he have no principle to direct his talents, his cleverness may lead him into sin and sorrow.

Clever men have not always been the most useful, nor are clever boys of necessity the most promising. A little principle is worth a great deal of cleverness any day of the year.

When a clever boy is brought to me, I ask these questions about him :—Does he fear God, honour his parents, obey his teachers, love his Bible, speak truth, act honestly, and behave kindly to those around him? If he does these things, I hear of his talents with pleasure: but if he does them not, his cleverness is to me as nothing.

Give me a boy of common understanding and good principles, who is teachable, patient, industrious, and persevering, and I will match him in the long-run against the cleverest lad you can find, deficient in these qualities.

Now mind, it is not cleverness that I undervalue, but unprofitable cleverness. I would have every boy clever if I could; I would have him say to himself, "Be my station high or low, with God's help I will do my duty therein with ability."

But then, let cleverness and usefulness go hand in hand together.

Old Barnaby.

FATHER WILLIAM.

"You are old, father William," the young man cried;
"The few locks that are left you are gray:
You are hale, father William, a hearty old man;
Now tell me the reason I pray."

"In the days of my youth," father William replied,
"I remembered that youth would fly fast;
And abused not my health and my vigour at first,
That I never might need them at last."

"You are old, father William," the young man cried,
"And pleasures with youth pass away;
And yet you lament not the days that are gone;
Now tell me the reason, I pray."

"In the days of my youth," father William replied,
"I remember'd that youth could not last;
I thought of the future, whatever I did,
That I never might grieve for the past."

"You are old, father William," the young man cried,
"And life must be hastening away;
You are cheerful, and love to converse upon death;
Now tell me the reason, I pray."

"I am cheerful, young man," father William replied,
"Let the cause thy attention engage:
In the days of my youth I remember'd my God,
And He hath not forgotten my age!"

Southey.

THE STORY OF SOME HOT WATER.

Mar'-quis	Im-prove'-ments	Re-sult'-ed
Ire'-land	En'-gine	Car'-riage
Con-clu'-ded	El'-e-vates	Fast'-en
Ex-per'-i-ment	Riv'-ets	Lo-co-mo'-tive
Ma-chine'	Pol'-ish-es	Rail'-roads

The story of some hot water is one of the most wonderful of stories. About two hundred years ago, a man, bearing the title of the Marquis of Worcester, was sitting, on a cold night, in a small mean room, before a blazing fire. This was in Ireland, and the man was a prisoner. A kettle of boiling water was on the fire, and he sat watching the steam, as it lifted the lid of the kettle and rushed out of the nose.

He thought of the power of the steam, and wondered what would be the effect if he were to fasten down the lid and stop up the nose. He concluded that the effect would be to burst the kettle. "How much power, then," thought he, "there must be in steam!" As soon as he was let out of prison he tried an experiment. "I have taken," he writes, "a cannon, and filled it three quarters full of water, stopping firmly up both the touch-hole and the mouth; and, having made a good fire under it, within twenty-four hours it burst, and made a great crack." After this, the marquis contrived a rude machine, which, by the power of steam, drove up water to the height of forty feet.

About one hundred years after this, a little boy, whose name was James Watt, and who lived in Scotland, sat one day looking at a kettle of boiling water, and holding a spoon before the steam that rushed out of the nose.

His aunt thought he was idle, and said, "Is it not a shame for you to waste your time so?" But James was not idle: he was thinking of the power of the steam in moving the spoon.

James grew to be a good and great man, and contrived those wonderful improvements in the steam-engine which have made it so useful in our day.

What will not the steam-engine do? It propels, it rows, it sculls, it screws, it elevates, it lowers, it lifts, it pumps, it drains, it waters, it draws, it pulls, it drives, it blasts, it digs, it grinds, it stamps, it punches, it sifts, it bolts, it presses, it picks, it hews, it cuts, it saws, it planes, it bores, it drills, it blows, it forges, it hammers, it files, it polishes, it rivets, it cards, it spins, it winds, it weaves, it coins, it prints; and it does more things than I can think of. If it could speak, it might say:

"I blow the bellows, I forge the steel,
I manage the mill and the mint;
I hammer the ore, and turn the wheel,
And the news that you read I print."

In the year 1807 Robert Fulton, an American, put

the first steam-boat on the Hudson river, and in 1829 a locomotive steam-carriage went over a railroad in England.

And this is the story of some hot water! From so small a beginning as the steam of a tea-kettle resulted the steam-engine, the steam-boat, and the locomotive engine, by which the trains of carriages are moved with such speed on our railroads!

Learn what the power of thought will do. How many men had looked at kettles of boiling water, but how few thought of the force of the steam, and the good uses to which it might be turned.

Constable's Series.

WHANG, THE MILLER.

Nat′-u-ral-ly	Ac-qui-si′-tions	Mat′-tock
Av-a-ri′-cious	Af′-flu-ence	Un-der-mine′
In′-ti-mate	Re-flec′-tions	Rap′-tures
Ac-quaint′-ed	As-si-du′-i-ty	Af-fair′
Fru-gal′-i-ty	Cus′-tom-ers	Ag′-o-ny
Con-tem′-plate	Mon′-strous	Oc-ca′-sion
Sat-is-fac′-tion	Foun-da′-tion	Treas′-ure

Whang, the miller, was naturally avaricious; nobody loved money better than he, or more respected those that had it. When people would talk of a rich man in company, Whang would say, "I know him very well; he and I have been long acquainted; he and I are intimate." But if ever a poor man was mentioned he had not the least knowledge of the man: he might be very well for aught he knew; but he was not fond of making many acquaintances, and loved to choose his company. Whang, however, with all his eagerness for riches was poor. He had nothing but the profits of his mill to support him; but though these were small, they were certain; while it stood and went he was sure of eating, and his frugality was such that he every day laid some money by, which he would at intervals count and contemplate with much satisfaction. Yet still his acquisitions were not equal to his desires; he only found himself above want, whereas he desired to be possessed of affluence. One day, as he was indulging these wishes, he was informed that a neighbour of his had found a pan of money under ground, having dreamed of it three nights running before. These tidings were daggers to the heart of poor Whang. "Here am I," says he, "toiling and moiling from morning to night for a few paltry farthings, while neighbour Thanks only goes quietly to bed, and dreams himself into thousands before morning. O that I could dream like him! With what pleasure would I dig round the pan! how slyly would I carry it home! not even my wife should see me: and then, oh, the pleasure of thrusting one's hand into a heap of gold up to the elbow!" Such reflections only served to make the miller unhappy: he discontinued his former assiduity; he was quite disgusted with small gains, and his customers began to forsake him. Every day he repeated the wish, and every night laid himself down in order to dream. Fortune, that was for a long time unkind, at last, however, seemed to smile upon his distresses, and indulged him with the wished-for vision. He dreamed, that under a certain part of the foundation of his mill there was concealed a monstrous pan of gold and diamonds, buried deep in the ground, and covered with a large flat stone. He concealed his good luck from every person, as is usual in money-dreams, in order to have the vision repeated the two succeeding nights, by which he should be certain of its truth. His wishes in this also were answered; he still dreamed of the same pan of money in the very same place.

Now, therefore, it was past a doubt: so getting up early the third morning, he repaired alone, with a mattock in his hand to the mill, and began to undermine that part of the wall which the vision directed. The first omen of success that he met was a broken ring; digging still deeper, he turned up a house-tile, quite new and entire. At last, after much digging, he came to a broad flat stone, but then so large that it was beyond man's strength to remove it. "There!" cried he in raptures to himself, "here it is; under this stone there is room for a very large pan of diamonds indeed. I must e'en go home to my wife and tell her the whole affair, and get her to assist me in turning it up." Away, therefore, he goes, and acquaints his wife with every circumstance of their good fortune. Her raptures on this occasion may easily be imagined: she flew round his neck and embraced him in an agony of joy; but those transports, however, did not allay their eagerness to know the exact sum; returning, therefore, together to the place where Whang had been digging, there they found—not, indeed, the expected treasure—but the mill, their only support, undermined and fallen!

Oliver Goldsmith.

CONTENTED JOHN.

One honest John Tomkins, a hedger and ditcher,
Although he was poor, did not want to be richer;
For all such vain wishes in him were prevented,
By a fortunate habit of being contented.

Though cold was the weather, or dear was the food,
John never was found in a murmuring mood;
For this he was constantly heard to declare,—
What he could not prevent he would cheerfully bear.

"For why should I grumble and murmur?" he said;
"If I cannot get meat, I can surely get bread;
And though fretting may make my calamities deeper,
It never can cause bread and cheese to be cheaper."

If John was afflicted with sickness or pain,
He wished himself better, but did not complain,
Nor lie down and fret in despondence and sorrow,
But said, that he hoped to be better to-morrow.

If any one wronged him or treated him ill,
Why, John was good-natured and sociable still;
For he said, that revenging the injury done
Would be making two rogues when there need be but one.

And thus honest John, though his station was humble,
Passed through this sad world without even a grumble;
And I wish that some folks, who are greater and richer,
Would copy John Tomkins the hedger and ditcher.

Jane Taylor.

THE RICH AND THE POOR.

As-sist′-ance	Pur′-chase	Su-perb′
Eq′-ui-page	Har′-ness	Man-u-fac′-tu-rers
Bom-ba-sin′	Liv′-er-y	Vex-a′-tion
Coun′-te-nance	Lux′-u-ries	Man′-sion
Cha-grined′	Com-mu′-ni-cate	Spin′-dles
Man-u-fac′-to-ry	Crock′-ery	Pros′-pect
Coach′-mak-er	To-bac′-co	Scare′-crow
Live′-li-hood	Ex-cep′-tion	Ar′-gu-ment

In the days of the fairies, John Hopkins, a poor labourer who had a large family to support upon scanty wages, applied to a Fairy for assistance. "Here am I half starving," said he, "while my landlord rides about in a fine carriage: it is hard that the rich should be allowed to spend money on luxuries, which might supply us poor men with bread."—"It is a pitiable case," replied the Fairy; "and I am ready to do all in my power to assist you. Shall I, by a stroke of my wand, destroy all the handsome equipages, fine clothes, and dainty dishes, which offend you?"—"Since you are so very obliging," said John, "it would be better to destroy all luxuries whatever; for if you destroy only those you mention, the rich will soon provide others in their place."

No sooner said than done. The good-natured Fairy waved her wand; and, wonderful to behold! the superb mansion of the landlord instantly shrunk into a thatched cottage, the gay apparel of its inmates changed into coarse clothing, the green-house plants became cabbages, and the pinery produced potatoes. John was profuse in his thanks; but the fairy stopped him short, "Return to me at the end of the week," said she; "it will be time enough to thank me when you can judge how far I have really obliged you."

Delighted with his success, John hastened to communicate the happy tidings to his wife. But she did not receive him with the joy he expected; for, on having gone to dress herself in her bombasin gown (it being Sunday), she beheld it changed to a homely stuff; and, to vex her yet more, she saw her china tea-pot, on which she set no small store, turned into crockery ware. John hummed and hawed as he observed her woful countenance, and, in order to console himself, called for his pipe. The goodwife ran to fetch it, when, lo and behold! the pipes and tobacco were all dissolved and gone. Poor John felt greatly chagrined, and said to himself, "What a fool I was not to desire the Fairy to meddle with the luxuries of the rich only! I will return to her at the end of the week, and beg her to make an exception in favour of the poor." This thought consoled him for a while, but, long before the end of the week, poor John had abundant cause to repent all he had done. His brother, who was employed in a silk manufactory, was, with all the other weavers, turned out of work; for the silk had disappeared, and the manufacturers, with ruin staring them in the face, had dismissed their workmen. John, still hoping to see great changes for the better soon, received his starving brother into his house. Next day, his eldest son returned home from the coachmaker with whom he worked, because there was no more coach-work—all the carriages being changed into carts and waggons. John well nigh groaned with vexation. "It is, however, fortunate for me," said he, "that I earn my livelihood as a labourer in the field. Corn and hay, thank God! are not luxuries; and I, at least shall not be thrown out of work."

In a few days, however, the landlord, on whose estate he worked, walked into the cottage. "John!" said he, "you are an honest, hard-working man, and I am sorry you should come to distress; but I have no more work for you, for I do not mean to cultivate my land any longer."—"Bless your honour, that would be a sad pity! Such fine meadows, and such corn! Cannot you sell your corn and hay as before?—*they* are not luxuries."—"No," replied the landlord, "I am now living on the produce of the few fields which I am able myself with the help of my sons, to cultivate; and why take the trouble to cultivate more? for since there are no luxuries to purchase, I want no more money than to buy the homely clothes which I and my family now wear."

Poor John was now reduced to despair; and when the week had expired, he hastened to the Fairy, and implored her to reverse the fatal decree, and to bring back things to what they had been before. The light wand once more waved in the air; and immediately the stately mansion rose from the lowly cottage; the heavy teams began to prance and snort till they became fine horses with showy harness: but, most of all, it was delightful to see the turned-off workmen running to their looms and their spindles, and every thing again offering a prospect of work, and wages, and comfort.

John grew wise by this lesson, and whenever any one complained of the hardness of the times, and laid it to the score of the expenses of the rich, took upon him to prove that the poor were gainers, not losers, by the luxuries of the rich. One night at the public-house, Bob Scarecrow, who was one of the listeners, cried out, "are you quite sure, John, that the poor are always gainers by luxuries? I know the contrary, to my cost. The young lord whom I served as gamekeeper set no bounds to his extravagance, until he had not a farthing left; and then his huntsman, his hounds, his gamekeeper, and his laced livery-servants were all sent off together! Now, I should be glad to know, John, whether *we* lost our places because there was too much luxury, or too little?" John felt that there was some truth in what Bob said, but was not fully convinced till Bob had finished his argument thus: "suppose that every man of substance were to spend his all, and come to ruin, a pretty plight we poor folks should be in; it is only when the rich live with prudence, and spend only what they can afford, that they can continue to keep us in employment."

John now went home, satisfied that the expenses of the rich would not harm the poor, unless these expenses first harmed the rich themselves. No bad safeguard! thought he; and as he trudged on, pondering it in his mind, he came to this conclusion—that the rich and the poor have but one and the same interest, and that the comforts of the poor are derived from the wealth of the rich.

Mrs. Marcet.

FROST—SNOW—ICE.

Prin′-ci-pal-ly	Tem′-per-a-ture	Liq′-uids
Phe-nom′-e-non	Gla′-ci-ers	Ar-ti-fi′-cial
Proc′-ess	Av′-a-lanch-es	Chem′-ists
Ac-cu′-mu-lates	At′-mos-phere	Ex-am′-ple
Ice′-bergs	Daz′-zling	Ther-mom′-e-ter
Floes	Veg-e-ta′-tion	Prep-a-ra′-tions

When the heat of the air falls below the freezing point, which it does principally from the weakness of the sun's rays in winter, the phenomenon of frost, or freezing ensues. Freezing is a process by which water is changed into ice. When the heat of the air rises above the freezing point, the ice begins to melt. In freezing, water expands or swells into a greater bulk, and in so doing it often bursts vessels, and even breaks up great pieces of rock in which it may have been confined. Ice is about one-ninth lighter than water, and hence it always floats on the surface. It frequently accumulates in vast masses in the polar seas, and is then known by such names as icebergs, floes, and ice-islands. In lofty regions, and on the tops of mountains, where the temperature seldom or never rises above the freezing point, ice and snow accumulate in masses, which, when they slide down, are known by the name of glaciers; fragments of them, called avalanches, sometimes descend with great violence into the valleys below, destroying trees, herds, and cottages.

When the heat of the air is below the freezing point, vapours become frozen, and fall to the earth in the form of snow. Rain-drops, frozen in their descent through a cold portion of the atmosphere, form hail. When the descending flakes of snow come into a temperature above the freezing point as they approach the earth, they are apt to melt, and, in such a case, fall in the shape of eet, which is half-melted snow. Light vapours, such ; dews and mists, which have been frozen during the ight, fall to the earth and form hoar-frost.

Snow is almost always of a dazzling white colour. Then it accumulates on the ground in winter, it is seful in keeping the earth at a moderate degree of ıld; for, where the snow lies, the temperature of the round beneath seldom descends below the freezing oint, which is by no means severe. The germs of egetation are thus kept alive in certain cold countries, here they would otherwise perish.

All liquids do not freeze at the same temperature. or example, olive oil freezes at fifty, water at thirty-vo, milk at thirty, and quicksilver not till the tempera-ıre is as low as thirty-nine degrees below zero. There e several artificial modes of producing intense cold, st as there are of producing heat. The most common ethod is by what are called freezing mixtures; pounded e and common salt, and new-fallen snow and salt, are ıch mixtures; they will reduce a thermometer placed in ıem several degrees below zero. These mixtures are ıed for cooling wines and liquors, and also by chemists some of their preparations.

Chambers's Lessons in Science.

THE FROST.

The frost looked forth one still clear night,
And whispered, "Now I shall be out of sight;
So through the valley and over the height,
In silence I'll take my way.
I will not go on like that blustering train,
The wind and the snow, the hail and the rain,
Who make so much bustle and noise in vain,
But I'll be as busy as they."

Then he flew to the mountain and powdered its crest:
He lit on the trees, and their boughs he drest
In diamond beads—and over the breast
  Of the quivering lake, he spread
A coat of mail that need not fear
The downward point of many a spear,
That he hung on a margin far and near,
  Where a rock could rear its head.

He went to the window of those who slept,
And over each pane, like a fairy crept;
Wherever he breathed, wherever he stepp'd,
  By the light of the moon were seen
Most beautiful things,—there were flowers and trees;
There were bevies of birds and swarms of bees;
There were cities with temples, and towers, and these
  All pictured in silver sheen!

But he did one thing that was hardly fair;
He peeped in at the cupboard, and finding there
That all had forgotten for him to prepare,
  "Now just to set them a thinking,
I'll bite this basket of fruit," said he,
"This costly pitcher I'll burst in three;
And this glass of water they 've left for me,
  Shall 'tchick' to tell them I 'm drinking."

H. F. Gould

WINTER NIGHT.

There 's a sough in the air, and the heavens are brown,
I think our old friend must be travelling down;
Ay, yonder 's a flake! Ho, young people, ho!
Come to the window and welcome the snow.
There are the pioneers, sailing around,
Not very sure of the ugly black ground;

Iere come the myriads, rather more quickly,
'he eye is bewildered, they float down so thickly.
Llas, the poor lilac! alas, the laburnum!
Iow soon into ghost-trees these mad fellows turn 'em!
Twill be a true fall this—thronger and thronger!
Vork away, Winter;—we'll look out no longer.

Snow searches well,—it may enter the mind,—
So, to defend ourselves, down with the blind!
Close both the shutters! Well said, sister dear!
Ve will leave a bit open, the passer to cheer.
Break up the fire, James! There is a blazer!
See how you 've made the walls laugh, Master Fraser!
Your 'broidery, Margaret! Mary, your knitting!
Everything ready and right for a sitting;
All the doors shut now? I 'm in my glory!
n with your chairs, and I'll read you a story.

Allan Park Paton.

JACK FROST.

A mischievous but merry Wight
Came from the north one winter night,
And pranks performed so very queer,
You 'll scarce believe them when you hear.

As o'er the fields he deftly sped,
The grass grew crisp beneath his tread;
The dew-drops, as they met his eye,
Shrunk into globules white and dry;
And to the air, where'er he went,
His breath a piercing keenness lent.

A waterfall stood in his way,
Busy with noise, and bright with spray;
"Ho! brawler," said he, "is it right,
To work and roar at dead of night?

You must no longer clamour so
When all besides a-slumbering go."
He said, and the obedient linn
Stood still, and hushed its clamorous din;
And what was water, in a trice
Stiffened into a sheet of ice.

A dairy-farm he reached; and strange
It was to mark the instant change:
The milk, the butter, and the cream
Grew solid like the frozen stream;
And from the milkmaid's cheek the rose
Fled with its blushes to her nose.

Next to the town he took his way,
Which sleeping in the moonlight lay;
And though he came and went unseen,
His feats soon told where he had been.
The watchmen, lounging on their beat
Took to "quick march," to give them heat;
The streets, begrimed with mud before,
Grew hard and sheen as marble-floor;
No pump, or water-pipe, or well,
But felt the mastery of his spell:
The very houses he swept through—
The roofs he powdered with hoar-dew,—
And every window pictured o'er
With forestry grotesque and hoar:—
"Ho! ho!" he said, "I'll let them see,
None of them all can paint like me."

At last he thought, presumptuous elf!
To vent his mischief on myself;
So, feeling certain of his game,
Into my quiet room he came,
But, let me tell you, Jacky Frost
Reckoned for once without his host.

I sat me there in warm attire,
With shutters closed and blazing fire;
And when he rush'd at me in spite,
Intent to freeze me and frost-bite,
I thawed his beard, and with a kick
Despatched him up the chimney quick.

Allan Park Paton.

WHEAT.

Cul-ti-va'-tion	Mum'-mies	Tre-men'-dous-ly
Nu-tri'-tious	Em-balmed'	Fash'-ion-a-ble
Mac-ca-ro'-ni	Ex-trav'-a-gant-ly	Pop-u-la'-tion
Pro-duc'-tive	Priv'-i-lege	Con'-i-cal
In'-dus-try	Glu'-ten	Man-da-rins'

Wheat, the staff of life, is the most important to man of all the grasses. It came to us from the East, but it is so altered, and improved by cultivation, that it cannot be traced to any species growing wild. The reason wheat is so valuable is because it contains a great quantity of glue; or, as it is called, gluten, which is very nutritious, and almost as strengthening as beef and mutton. But, besides gluten, it contains also starch, for starch is found in nearly every kind of plant: it is intended for the nourishment of the seed, and is deposited like a store of food all round it. When the gluten is washed free from starch, it is made into long pipes, and sold in the market under the name of maccaroni. Maccaroni is the favourite food of the lower classes in Italy, who can buy it by the yard, at the corners of the street.

Wheat is very productive, but the abundance of the crop depends very much on the nature of the soil, and the skill and industry of the farmer.

But besides its productive power, a grain of wheat

may lie a great number of years unset, without being injured. The mummies in the Egyptian tombs, have, some of them been embalmed with ears of corn in their hands. This corn has remained there for ages, I might say, for thousands of years, and yet the tiny germ, of which I have been speaking, has not perished. On being planted it has sprung up, and again sent up its golden ears.

In England, in the olden times, wheaten bread was not so abundant as it is now, and very often a season of feasting was succeeded by a long period of fasting. When the new corn first came in, people used it extravagantly, and not even a beggar would eat anything but wheaten bread. The consequence was, it soon came to an end, and all the rest of the year everybody had to live upon cakes made of oats or rye.

In Cumberland the quantity of wheat was so small, that only the rich could afford it by way of a treat at Christmas. In those days the corn used to be ground at home by the mistress of the house in a hand-mill, called a quern. Windmills and watermills had both been invented, but the farmer seldom made use of them, for if he did, he was obliged by law to grind at his landlord's mill, and to give him a good part of the corn for the privilege of grinding the rest.

In Tuscany, the straw of a certain kind of wheat is used for making hats and bonnets, which are very fashionable, and are called Leghorns, after the name of a city in Tuscany.

The population in the South of China, use no other covering for the head in summer, but a conical straw hat, and as some of the mandarins have them made with tremendously wide brims, the quantity of straw platted is enormous.

Not only straw hats, but also shoes and slippers of the same material are worn *both by rich and poor in*

Japan. They are not very durable, but they cost a mere trifle, and may be bought in every town and village.

The Observing Eye.

NEW ZEALAND CHIEFS AND WHEAT.

Zea'-land	Flour'-ish-ing	En-raged'
Mis'-sion-a-ry	Im-pa'-tient	Pa'-tient-ly
Di-rec'-tions	Pos'-si-bly	In-dus'-tri-ous

I can tell you a story about the wheat being sown in New Zealand. A Missionary once made a present to some chiefs of a portion of wheat, and told them that if they sowed it in the ground, it would grow up, and they might then make it into bread. They sowed it according to his directions, and the wheat sprang up, and looked very flourishing. But before the grain could possibly ripen, they began to be impatient for the crop, which they expected would be underground, and something like potatoes. They searched for it at the root of the stem, but as no corn was to be found, they were so enraged, that they pulled up all their wheat, and burnt it. One chief, however, who knew better than his companions, waited more patiently, and allowed his corn to ripen. The other chiefs laughed at him, but he took no notice of their taunts, and by and bye his corn got ripe and was thrashed. The chiefs were now convinced that the grain grew at the top, and not at the bottom of the stem, but still they did not believe it could ever make bread.

Soon after, the missionary presented the industrious native with a handmill to grind his corn, which he received with great delight. He set to work to grind the wheat before his companions, who danced and shouted for joy when they saw the flour. He immediately made a cake and baked it in a frying pan, and so fully proved to them that wheat could be made into bread.

Id.

THE PILGRIMS AND THEIR PITCHERS.

Al-a-bas′-ter	Cau′-tious-ly	Cour-a′-geous
Ex′-qui-site-ly	Ac-cost′-ed	Pearl′-y
Del′-i-cate	Work′-man-ship	Pre′-cincts
Com-po′-sure	A-muse′-ments	Skil′-ful-ly

It was long ago, and somewhere in the Eastern clime. The king came into the garden and called the children round him. He led them up to a sunny knoll, and a leafy arbour on its summit. And when they had all sat down, he said, "You see far down the river, and hanging as on the side of the hill, yonder palace? It is a palace, though here it looks so little and far away. But when you reach it you will find it a larger and sweeter home than this: and when you come you will find that I have got there before you. And when you arrive at the gate, that they may know that you belong to me, and may let you in, here is what each of you must take with him." And he gave to each of the children a most beautiful alabaster jar—a little pitcher so exquisitely fashioned that you were almost afraid to touch it, so pure that you could see the day-light through it, and with delicate figures raised on its sides. "Take this, and carry it carefully. Walk steadily and the journey will soon be over."

But they had not gone far, before they forgot. One was running carelessly and looking over his shoulder, when his foot stumbled, and as he fell full length on the stony path, the pitcher was shivered in a thousand pieces; and one way and another, long, long before they reached the palace, they had broken all their pitchers. When this happened, I may mention what some of them did. Some grew sulky, and knowing that it was of no use to go forward without the token, they began to shatter the fragments still smaller. They dashed the broken sherds among the stones, and stamped with their feet: and then they said, "Why trouble ourselves about this palace?

It is far away, and here is a pleasant spot. We will just stay here and play."

And so they began to play. Another could not play, but sat wringing his hands, and weeping bitterly. Another grew pale at first, but recovered his composure a little, on observing that his pitcher was not broken so bad as some others. There were three or four large pieces, and these he put together as well as he could. It was a broken pitcher that could hold no water, but by a little care he could keep it together; and so he gathered courage, and began to walk along more cautiously.

Just then a voice accosted the weeping boy, and looking up he saw a very lovely form, with a sweet and pleasant countenance—such a countenance as is accustomed to be happy, though something for the present has made it sad. And in his hand he held just such a pitcher as the little boy had broken, only the workmanship was more exquisite, and the colours were as bright as the rainbow round the stranger's head. "You may have this," he said; "it is better than the one you have lost, and though it is not the same, they will know it at the gate." The little mourner could scarcely believe that it was really meant for him; but the kind looks of the stranger encouraged him. He held out his hand for the stranger's vase, and gave a sob of joyful surprise when he found it his own. He began his journey again, and you would have liked to see how tenderly he carried his treasure, and how carefully he picked his steps, and how sometimes, when he gave another look at it, the tear would fill his eye, and he lifted up his happy, thankful face to heaven.

The stranger made the same offer to the playing boys, but by this time they were so bent on their new amusements, that they did not care for it. Some saucy children said, he might lay his present down and leave it there if he liked, and they would take it when they wanted it.

He passed away, and spoke to the boy who was carrying the broken pitcher. At first he would have denied that it was broken, but the traveller's clear glance had already seen it all; and so he told him, "You had better cast it away, and have this one in its stead." The boy would have been very glad to have this new one, but to throw away the relics of his own was what he could never think of. They were his chief dependence every time he thought of the journey's end; so he thanked the stranger, and clasped his fragments firmer. The boy with the gift pitcher and this other reached the precincts of the palace about the same time. They stood for a little and looked on. They noticed some of the bright-robed inhabitants going out and in, and every time they passed the gate, they presented such a token as they themselves had once got from the king, but had broken so long ago.

The boy who had accepted the kind stranger's present, now went forward, and held it up; and whether it was the light glancing on it from the pearly gate, I cannot tell, but at that instant its owner thought that it had never looked so fair. He who kept the gate seemed to think the same, for he gave a friendly smile, as much as to say, "I know who gave you that;" and immediately the door was lifted up and let the little pilgrim in. The boy with the broken pitcher now began to wish that his choice had been the same, but there was no help for it now. He adjusted the fragments as skilfully as he could, and trying to look courageous, carried them in both his hands. But he who kept the gate was not to be deceived. He shook his head, and there was that sorrow in his look which leaves no hope. The bearer of the broken pitcher still held fast his useless sherds, and lingered long. But no one took any notice of him, or felt the smallest pity for him; and though he made many efforts, every time he approached the door it seemed of itself to shut again. *Hamilton's Happy Home.*

THE WIDOW OF NAIN.

Slow from the darkened city's gates
  Forth came a funeral train;
It was a mother's only son,
  A widowed one's of Nain.

Oh! bitter is the Dead Sea brine
  And deep, deep is its flow;
But bitterer are a mother's tears,
  Deeper a mother's woe.

One only hope she had on earth,
  That only hope is fled;
In vain the sun now shines for her,—
  Her beautiful is dead.

The flower that fades in winter's wind
  In spring again will bloom;
But what can cheer the mourner's lot,
  Whose heart is in the tomb?

The Lord drew near with pitying gaze,
  He saw the sorrowing one;
"Weep not," He said; and from the dead
  Restored to life her son.

Now Nain was glad, and songs of joy
  Rang all the city round;
Our dead one is alive again,
  Our lost one—he is found!

Pencillings in Palestine.

———o———

THE STORM.

Mark vi. 47—51.

Fear was within the tossing bark,
When stormy winds grew loud;
And waves came rolling high and dark,
And the tall mast was bowed.

And men stood breathless in their dread,
And baffled in their skill;
But One was there, who rose and said
To the wild sea, " Be still ! "

And the wind ceased—it ceased—that word,
Passed through the gloomy sky;
The troubled billows knew their Lord,
And sank beneath his eye.

And slumber settled on the deep,
And silence on the blast,
As when the righteous falls asleep,
When death's fierce throes are past.

Thou that didst rule the angry hour,
And tame the tempest's mood,
Oh! send Thy spirit forth in power,
O'er our dark souls to brood!

Thou that didst bow the billow's pride,
Thy mandates to fulfil—
So speak to passion's raging tide,
Speak and say, " Peace, be still ! "

Mrs. Hemans.

——o——

SELFISHNESS.—Part I.

Daugh′-ters	Ar-ith-met′-i-cal	Be-moan′
Glut′-ton	E-ter′-ni-ty	Hid′-e-ous
Mis′-sion-a-ry	Ex-is′-tence	Self′-ish-ness
Rec′-ip-e	Eth′-ics	Ser′-mon
Res-o-lu′-tion	Med′-i-cine	Pos-ses′-sions

If I were asked what kind of young people were the most unhappy, what do you think my answer would be? The poor, or the sick, or the ugly, or the stupid? Oh no! these may all be happy and useful. It is only the *selfish*, those that "seek their own," that are never satisfied. Like the daughters of the horse-leech, they cry, "Give, give," but never say, "It is enough;" for it would seem that the more people seek their own happiness, the less they get of it. It has been said, "The *self*, the *I*, the *me*, and the like, all belong to the Evil Spirit," and we know that he is not a *happy* spirit. No human being can be really happy who is not giving or trying to give happiness to others. The sixpence added to the hoard of the little selfish miser, or spent by the glutton in the cake-shop, may give a moment's pleasure, but will leave no pleasant thoughts behind; while the sixpence, part of which is dropped into the missionary box, part given to feed a poor starving child, part given to purchase a biscuit or an orange to please the little sister, will send the happy spender of it on her way, bright-faced and light-hearted.

Here is a "Recipe for making every day happy." If each of us were to follow it, there would soon be an end of our many listless, disagreeable, unhappy days. "When you rise in the morning, form a resolution to make the day a happy one to a fellow-creature. It is easily done; a left-off garment to the man who needs it, a kind word to the sorrowful, an encouraging expression to the striving; trifles, in themselves light as air, will do it, at least for the twenty-four hours; and if you are young, depend upon it, it will tell when you are old; and if you are old, rest assured it will send you gently and happily down the stream of human time towards eternity. By the most simple arithmetical sum, look at the result: you send one person, only one, happily through the day; that is, three hundred and sixty-five in the course of the year; and supposing you live for forty years only after you commence that course of medicine, you have made 14,600 human beings happy, at all events, for a time. Now, worthy reader, is not this simple! It is too short for a sermon, too homely for ethics, too easily accomplished for you to say, 'I would if I could.'"

It is a curious fact that selfish people, however disagreeable they may make themselves by their selfishness, are always the first to bemoan the existence of this fault in others, and perhaps you are each quite ready to remember how selfish Dick, and Harry, and Mary, and Susan are; but ah! my dear young friends, look at home—look into your own hearts, with their curious depths which you scarcely understand, or perhaps never tried to understand, and there you will find an ugly black spot—perhaps a small one. It will not long be very small, however, if you go on "seeking your own;" it will grow and grow, till at last the heart is one mass of black, hideous selfishness! Try to conquer this besetting-sin. When you have a little time, think what you can do with it to please or help others; when you have a little money, think whom you can comfort and assist with it; when you have not much of the one, and none of the other, still think whose heart you can gladden with kind words and kind looks. Teach your hearts to think first of others, and last of yourselves. Learn to give up your own pleasure, your own way, your own possessions, that you may know how much "more blessed it is to give than to receive." Remember that the Lord of heaven and earth "pleased not Himself," and that his command is, "Look not every one on his own things, but every one also on the things of others."

SELFISHNESS.—Part II.

Com-pla′-cent-ly	Dim′-pled	Ca-pa′-cious
Su-pe′-ri-or	Pes-ti-len′-tial	Foun′-tain
Ac-tiv′-i-ty	A′-gue	Bap′-tism
Stag′-nant	In′-cense	Fore′-sight

Listen to this beautiful little story or fable, called the "Selfish Pool, and what befell it."

"See that little fountain yonder, away yonder in the distant mountain, shining like a thread of silver through the thick copse, and sparkling like a diamond in its healthful activity. It is hurrying on with tinkling feet to bear its tribute to the river. See, it passes a stagnant pool, and the pool hails it. 'Whither away, master streamlet?' 'I am going to the river, to bear this cup of water God has given me.' 'Ah, you are very foolish for that; you'll need it before the summer is over. It has been a backward spring, and we shall have a hot summer to pay for it; you will dry up then.' 'Well,' says the streamlet, 'if I am to die so soon, I had better work while the day lasts. If I am likely to lose this treasure from the heat, I had better do good with it while I have it.' So on it went, blessing and rejoicing in its course. The pool smiled complacently at its own superior foresight, and husbanded all its resources, letting not a drop steal away. Soon the midsummer heat came down, and it fell upon the little stream. But the trees crowded to its brink, and threw out their sheltering branches over it in the day of adversity, for it brought refreshment and life to them; and the sun peeped through the branches, and smiled complacently upon its dimpled face, and seemed to say, 'It is not in my heart to harm you;' and the birds sipped its silver tide, and sang its praises; the flowers breathed their perfume upon its bosom; the beasts of the field loved to linger by its banks; the husbandman's eye always sparkled with joy as he looked upon the line of verdant beauty that marked its course through his fields and meadows; and so on it went, blessing and blessed of all. And where was the prudent pool? Alas! in its inglorious inactivity, it grew sickly and pestilential; the beasts of the fields put their lips to it, but turned away without drinking; the breezes stooped and kissed it by *mistake*, but caught the malaria, in the contact, and carried the ague through the region, and the inhabitants caught it, and had to move away; and at last Heaven, in mercy to man, smote it with a hotter breath, and dried it up. But did not the little stream exhaust itself? Oh no! God saw to that. It emptied its full cup into the river, and the river bore it to the sea, and the sea welcomed it, and the sun smiled upon the sea, and the sea sent up its incense to greet the sun, and the clouds caught in their capacious bosoms the incense from the sea, and the winds, like waiting steeds, caught the chariots of the clouds and bore them away—away to the very mountain that gave the little fountain birth, and there they tipped the brimming cup, and poured the grateful baptism down; and so God saw to it that the little fountain, though it gave so fully and so freely, never ran dry. And if God so bless the fountain, will He not also bless you, my friends, if, 'as ye have freely received, ye also freely give?'"

M. M. Gordon.

—o—

THE WICKED BISHOP.

The summer and autumn had been so wet
That in winter the corn was growing yet,
'Twas a piteous sight to see all around
The grain lie rotting on the ground.

Every day the starving poor
Crowded around Bishop Hatto's door,
For all the neighbourhood could tell
His granaries were furnished well.

At last Bishop Hatto appointed a day
To quiet the poor without delay;
He bade them to his great Barn repair,
And they should have food for the winter there.

Rejoiced such tidings good to hear,
The poor folk flocked from far and near;
So the great Barn was full as it could hold
Of women and children, and young and old.

Then when he saw it could hold no more,
Bishop Hatto he made fast the door;
And while for mercy with shrieks they call,
He set fire to the Barn and burnt them all.

" A rare and excellent bonfire! " quoth he,
" And the country is greatly obliged to me,
For ridding it in these times forlorn
Of Rats that only consume the corn."

So then to his palace returned he,
And he sat down to supper merrily,
And he slept that night like an innocent man;—
But Bishop Hatto never slept again.

In the morning as he entered the hall,
Where his picture hung against the wall,
A sweat like death all over him came,
For the rats had eaten it out of the frame.

As he looked, there came a man from his farm,
He had a countenance white with alarm;—
"I opened your granaries this morn,
And the rats had eaten all the corn."

Another came running presently,
And he was pale as pale could be;—
"Fly! my Lord Bishop, without delay,
Ten thousand Rats are coming this way."

"I'll go to my tower on the Rhine," quoth he,
"'Tis the safest place in Germany;
The walls are high and the shores are steep,
And the stream is strong and the water deep."

Bishop Hatto fearfully hastened away,
And he crossed the Rhine without delay,
And reached his tower, and barred with care
All the windows, doors, and loopholes there.

He laid him down and closed his eyes;—
But soon a scream made him arise,
He started and saw two eyes of flame
On his pillow from whence the screaming came.

He listened and looked:—it was only the Cat;
But the Bishop he grew more fearful for that,
For she sat screaming, mad with fear
At the Army of Rats that were drawing near.

For they have swum over the river so deep,
And they have climbed the shores so steep,

And up the tower their way is bent,
To do the work for which they were sent.

Down on his knees the Bishop fell,
And faster and faster his beads did he tell,
As louder and louder drawing near
The gnawing of their teeth he could hear.

And in at the windows and in at the door,
And down from the roof helter-skelter they pour,
From behind and before, from above and below,
And all at once to the Bishop they go.

They have whetted their teeth against the stones,
And now they pick the Bishop's bones;
They gnawed the flesh from every limb,
For they were sent to do judgment on him,

Southey.

THE INCHCAPE BELL.

No stir in the air, no stir in the sea,
The ship was still as ship might be:
Her sails from heaven received no motion,
Her keel was steady in the ocean.

Without either sign or sound of their shock,
The waves flowed over the Inchcape Rock;
So little they rose so little they fell,
They did not move the Inchcape Bell.

The worthy abbot of Aberbrothock
Had floated that bell on the Inchcape Rock;
On the waves of the storm it floated and swung,
And louder and louder it warning rung.

When the rock was hid by the tempest's swell,
The mariners heard the warning bell;
And then they knew the perilous rock,
And blest the priest of Aberbrothock.

The float of the Inchcape Bell was seen,
A darker speck on the ocean green:
Sir Ralph the Rover walked his deck,
And he fixed his eye on the darker speck.

His eye was on the bell and float:
Quoth he, "My men, put out the boat,
And row me to the Inchcape Rock,
And I 'll plague the priest of Aberbrothock."

The boat is lowered, the boatmen row,
And to the Inchcape Rock they go:
Sir Ralph bent over from the boat,
And cut the warning-bell from the float.

Down sank the bell with a gurgling sound,
The bubbles arose and burst around;
Quoth Sir Ralph, "The next who comes to this rock
Will not bless the priest of Aberbrothock."

Sir Ralph the Rover sailed away,
He scoured the seas for many a day;
And now, grown rich with plundered store,
He steers his course to Scotland's shore.

So thick a haze o'erspreads the sky,
They cannot see the sun on high:
The wind hath blown a gale all day,
At ev'ning it had died away.

"Canst hear," said one, "the breaker's roar?
For yonder, methinks, should be the shore;

Now where we are I cannot tell,
But I wish we could hear the Inchcape Bell."

They hear no sound, the swell is strong;
Though the wind hath fallen, they drift along,
Till the vessel strikes with a shivering shock—
O heavens! it is the Inchcape Rock!

Sir Ralph the Rover tore his hair,
He cursed himself in his despair;
But the waves rush in on every side,
And the vessel sinks beneath the tide.

Southey.

THE HEROIC SMITH.

He-ro′-ic	An′-vil	Fol′-low-ing
Ven′-om-ous	Hor′-ri-ble	As-sem′-bled
Riv′-et-ed	Con-fu′-sion	Cir′-cum-stance

The following circumstance took place about twenty years ago at a village in Germany, One afternoon a great number of the villagers were assembled in the large room of the inn. There was only one door to the room, and that stood open. The village blacksmith—a good-natured, pious, brave-hearted man—sat near the door, talking pleasantly with some of his neighbours in the room.

All at once a large dog came and stood right in the door-way. He was a great powerful beast, with fierce frightful look. His head hung down, his eyes were bloodshot, his great red tongue hung half out of his mouth, and his tail was dropped between his legs. As soon as the keeper of the inn saw him, he turned pale, and exclaimed, "Back, back! The dog is mad!" Then the women screamed, and there was great confusion in the room. There was no way out but by the door in which the dog stood, and no one could pass him without being bitten.

"Stand back my friends," cried the brave smith, "till I seize the dog; then burry out while I hold him. It is better that one should perish than all."

As he said this, he seized the foaming beast with an iron grasp, and dashed him on the floor. Then a terrible struggle followed. The dog bit furiously on every side in a most frightful manner. His long teeth tore the arms and thighs of the heroic smith, but he would not let go his hold. Unmindful of the great pain it caused, and the horrible death which he knew must follow, with the grasp of a giant he held down the snapping, biting, howling brute, till all his friends had escaped in safety. Then he flung the half strangled beast from him against the wall, and dripping with blood and venomous foam, he left the room and locked the door. The dog was shot through the window, but what became of the brave but unfortunate smith?

The friends whose lives he had saved at the expense of his own, stood round him weeping. "Be quiet, my friends," he said, "do not weep for me, I have only done my duty. When I am dead, think of me with love; and now pray for me that God will not let me suffer long, or too much. I know I shall become mad, but I will take care that no harm comes to you through me."

He went to his shop, and took a strong chain, one end of which he riveted with his own hands round his body, the other end he fastened round the anvil so strongly that no earthly power could loose it. He then looked round on his friends and said, "Now it's done. You are all safe, I can't hurt you. Bring me food while I am well, and keep out of my reach when I am mad! The rest I leave with God."

Nothing could save the brave smith. Madness soon seized him and he died after nine days of suffering. What a noble fellow! What a real hero that was!

Dr. Newton.

HUMANITY.

rem'-i-ties	Un-daunt'-ed	An'-swered
ev'-o-lent	Cour'-age	Cu-ri-os'-i-ty
ɔo-si'-tion	Trench'-es	Prompt'-ing
ıf-fi'-cient	Pres'-ent-ly	Mis'-er-y
es'-si-ties	Sol'-dier	Vi'-o-lent-ly
om-pensed	Flag'-on	As-ton'-ish-ment
-i-den'-tial	Gen'-er-ous	Duc'-ats
ɾi'-sions	Gal'-lant	Af-fec'-tion

ıring the retreat of the famous King Alfred at lney, in Somersetshire, after the defeat of his forces he Danes, the following circumstance happened, ı shows the extremities to which that great man ɾeduced, and gives a striking proof of his pious and ɾolent disposition. A beggar came to his little ɘ, and requested alms. His queen informed him they had only one small loaf remaining, which was ficient for themselves and their friends, who were abroad in quest of food, though with little hope of ss. But the king replied, " Give the poor Christian ıalf of the loaf. He that could feed five thousand five loaves and two fishes, can certainly make that of the loaf suffice for more than our necessities." rdingly, the poor man was relieved; and this noble f charity was soon recompensed by a providential of fresh provisions, with which his people returned.

ɾ Philip Sydney, at the battle near Zutphen, dis- d the most undaunted courage. He had two horses l under him; and, whilst mounting a third, was ıded by a musket-shot out of the trenches, which ɘ the bone of his thigh. He returned about a mile ı half on horseback to the camp; and being faint the loss of blood, and parched with thirst from the heat of the weather, he called for drink. It was presently brought him; but, as he was putting the vessel to his mouth, a poor wounded soldier, who happened to be carried along at that instant, looked up to it with wistful eyes. The gallant and generous Sydney took the flagon from his lips, just when he was going to drink, and delivered it to the soldier, saying, "Thy necessity is greater than mine."

Frederick, King of Prussia, one day rang his bell, and nobody answered, on which he opened the door, and found his page fast asleep in an elbow-chair. He advanced towards him, and was going to awaken him, when he perceived a letter hanging out of his pocket. His curiosity prompting him to know what it was, he took it out and read it. It was a letter from the young man's mother, in which she thanked him for having sent her part of his wages to relieve her in her misery, and finished with telling him that God would reward him for his dutiful affection. The king, after having read it, went back softly into his chamber, took a bag full of ducats, and slipped it with the letter into the page's pocket. Returning to his chamber, he rang the bell so violently that he awakened the page, who instantly made his appearance. "You have had a sound sleep," said the king. The page was at a loss how to excuse himself, and, putting his hand into his pocket by chance, to his utter astonishment he there found a purse of ducats. He took it out, turned pale, and looking at the bag, burst into tears without being able to utter a single word. "What is that?" said the king; "what is the matter?" "Ah, sire!" said the young man, throwing himself on his knees, "somebody seeks my ruin! I know nothing of this money which I have just found in my pocket!" "My young friend," replied Frederick, "God often does great things for us even in our sleep.

Send that to your mother, salute her on my part, and assure her that I will take care of both her and you."

Beauties of History.

THE WIND IN A FROLIC.

The wind one morning sprang up from sleep
Saying, " Now for a frolic! now for a leap!
Now for a mad-cap galloping chase!
I 'll make a commotion in every place!"

So it swept with a bustle right through a great town,
Cracking the signs and scattering down
Shutters; and whisking with merciless squalls,
Old women's bonnets and gingerbread stalls.
There never was heard a much lustier shout,
As the apples and oranges trundled about;
And the urchins that stand with their thievish eyes
For ever on watch, ran off each with a prize.

Then away to the fields it went, blustering and humming,
And the cattle all wondered what monster was coming;
It plucked by the tails the grave matronly cows,
And tossed the colts' manes all over their brows;
Till, offended at such an unusual salute,
They all turned their backs, and stood sulky and mute.

So on it went capering and playing its pranks,
Whistling with reeds on the broad river's banks,
Puffing the birds as they sat on the spray,
Or the traveller grave on the king's highway.
It was not too nice to hustle the bags
Of the beggar, and flutter his dirty rags;
'Twas so bold that it feared not to play its joke
With the doctor's wig or the gentleman's cloak.

Through the forest it roared and cried gaily, " Now
You sturdy old oaks, I 'll make you bow; "
And it made them bow without more ado,
Or it cracked their great branches through and through.

Then it rushed like a monster on cottage and farm,
Striking their dwellers with sudden alarm;
And they ran out like bees in a midsummer swarm:
There were dames with their'kerchiefs tied over their caps;
To see if their poultry were free from mishaps ;
The turkeys they gobbled, the geese screamed aloud,
And the hens crept to roost in a terrified crowd;
There was rearing of ladders, and logs were laid on,
Where the thatch from the roof threatened soon to be
gone.

But the wind had swept on, and had met in a lane
With a schoolboy, who panted and struggled in vain;
For it tossed him and twirled him, then passed and he
stood
With his hat in a pool and his shoes in the mud.

Then away went the wind in its holiday glee,
And now it was far on the billowy sea,
And the lordly ships felt its staggering blow,
And the little boats darted to and fro.
But lo ! it was night, and it sank to rest
On the sea-bird's rock in the gleaming west,
Laughing to think, in its frolicsome fun,
How little of mischief it had done.

William Howitt.

---o---

PERSEVERANCE.

King Bruce of Scotland flung himself down,
In a lonely mood to think;
'Tis true he was monarch, and wore a crown,
But his heart was beginning to sink.

For he had been trying to do a great deed,
To make his people glad;
He had tried and tried, but could not succeed,
And so he became quite sad.

He flung himself down to low despair,
As grieved as man could be,
And after a while he pondered there,
"I'll give it up," cried he.

Now just at the moment a spider dropped,
With its silken cobweb clew;
And the king in the midst of his thinking stopped,
To see what the spider would do.

'Twas a long way up to the ceiling dome,
And it hung by a rope so fine,
That how it would get to its cobweb home,
King Bruce could not divine.

It soon began to cling and crawl
Straight up with strong endeavour;
But down it came with a slipping sprawl,
As near to the ground as ever.

Up, up it ran, nor a second did stay,
To make the least complaint,
Till it fell still lower; and there it lay
A little dizzy and faint.

Its head grew steady—again it went,
And travelled a half yard higher;

'Twas a delicate thread it had to tread,
  And a road where its feet would tire.

Again it fell, and swung below;
  But up it quickly mounted,
Till up and down, now fast, now slow,
  Nine brave attempts were counted.

" Sure," said the king, " that foolish thing
  Will strive no more to climb,
When it toils so hard to reach and cling,
  And tumbles every time."

But up the insect went once more;
  Ah me! 'tis an anxious minute;
He 's only a foot from his cobweb door,
  Oh say, will he lose or win it ?

Steadily, steadily—inch by inch,
  Higher and higher he got,
And a bold little run at the very last pinch,
  Put him into the wished-for spot.

" Bravo, Bravo! " the king cried out;
  " All honour to those who try:
The spider up there defied despair;
  He conquered, and why should not I? "

And Bruce of Scotland braced his mind,
  And gossips tell the tale,
That he tried once more as he tried before,
  And that time he did not fail.

Pay goodly heed, all you who read,
  And beware of saying " I can't,"
'Tis a cowardly word, and apt to lead
  To idleness, folly, and want.

Eliza Cook.

ADMIRAL LORD NELSON (1758—1805).

Ad'-mi-ral	Hes-i-ta'-tion	De-pos'-it-ed
De-cep'-tion	Re-luc'-tance	Prin'-ci-ple
Va-ca'-tion	Cau'-tious-ly	Ob'-sta-cles
Hol'-i-days	Dis-suad'-ed	Ar'-gu-ments
Im-pas'-sa-ble	Con-sci-en'-tious	Fear'-less-ness

Horatio was a boy of a strong sense of fearlessness, and shrank from anything like deception or meanness. When he was between eight and nine years of age, he and his brother came home from school for the Christmas holidays. The happy vacation was soon over, but the deep snow remained on the roads for some days, and rendered them almost impassable. This was fine fun for the two boys, who thus enjoyed a few more holidays. But at length their father, with some hesitation, told them he thought they might venture to go the next day. Oh! how much they wished a heavy fall of snow would come in the night and keep them a little longer at their happy home. But no; the day proved fine, though cold, and the boys, with reluctance, mounted their ponies to go to school. "Now, remember, boys," said their kind father, as he wished them good-bye, "I expect you to *try* to reach your school. The snow has drifted a good deal, and the road may be impassable; in that case you must return. But if you can proceed with safety, I wish you to do so. Good-bye, my dear boys; remember, I trust to your sense of honour."

The boys set off, and no doubt hoped to find that the roads *were* impassable. Indeed, they had not proceeded more than two miles when William, the elder brother, declared he thought it dangerous to go on, and would have turned back had not the younger one urged him to continue. They went on, slowly and cautiously, till, about a mile further on, they found the snow had drifted very much on the road. William now again proposed returning, and again his brother dissuaded him from so doing. "You know, dear William," said the conscientious boy, "our father wished us to *try* to get to school. Besides, he trusted to our honour! we must try as much to get there as we should if it were our dear home to which we were going. Come, William, remember—our honour!" So on they went, and got over that difficulty, and the next; and though really the road in some parts was almost impassable, yet still it was not *quite* so; and though William, two or three times, proposed their returning home, yet his younger brother, by his arguments and example, encouraged him to proceed. "Remember, William! he trusted to our honour!" said the brave boy, as their little ponies slowly made their way through the snow, and at last deposited them, cold and tired, at the school.

And what do you think was the name of this fearless and noble boy, who thus at an early age, gave proof of the principle on which he acted through life, that, in spite of all obstacles, he would "*Do his duty?*" It was a name of which England became justly proud, and which is dear to every English heart—it was Horatio Nelson.

———o———

SECTION V.

—o—

THE SNOW-STORM.

Knolls	In′-no-cence	Res′-ig-na-tion
Ac-com′-pa-ni-ment	Be-nign′-ly	De-spair′
Con-stel-la′-tions	Sol′-i-ta-ry	Des′-pe-rate
Prov′-i-dence	Pas′-tor-al	In-sur-mount′-a-ble
In-ter′-mi-na-bly	In-ef-fec′-tu-al	Ex-er′-tion
In-sen-si-bil′-i-ty	E-ter′-ni-ty	Bar′-ri-er

Little Hannah Lee had left her master's house as soon as the rim of the great moon was seen by her eyes, that had been long anxiously watching it from the window, rising, like a joyful dream, over the gloomy mountain tops; and all by herself she tripped along beneath the beauty of the silent heaven. Still, as she kept ascending and descending the knolls that lay in the bosom of the glen, she sang to herself a song, a hymn, or a psalm, without the accompaniment of the streams, now all silent in the frost, and ever and anon she stopped to try to count the stars that lay in some more beautiful part of the sky, or gazed on the constellations that she knew, and called them, in her joy, by the names they bore among the shepherds. There were none to hear her voice or see her smiles, but the ear and eye of Providence. As on she glided, and took her looks from heaven, she saw her own little fireside—her parents waiting for her arrival—the Bible opened for worship—her own little room kept so neatly for her, with its mirror hanging by the window in which to braid her hair by the morning light—her bed prepared for her by her mother's hand—the primroses in her garden peeping through the snow—old Tray, who ever welcomed her home with his dim white eyes—the pony and the cow—friends all and inmates of that happy household. So stepped she along, while the snow-diamonds glittered around her feet, and the frost wove a wreath of lucid pearls round her forehead.

She had now reached the edge of the Black-moss, which lay half way between her master's and her father's dwelling, when she heard a loud noise coming down Glen Scrae, and in a few seconds she felt on her face some flakes of snow. She looked up the glen, and saw the snow-storm coming down fast as a flood. She felt no fears: but she ceased her song, and, had there been a human eye to look upon her there, it might have seen a shadow upon her face. She continued her course, and felt bolder and bolder every step that brought her nearer to her parents' house. But the snow-storm had now reached the Black-moss, and the broad line of light that had lain in the direction of her home was soon swallowed up, and the child was in utter darkness. She saw nothing but the flakes of snow, interminably intermingled and furiously wafted in the air close to her head; she heard nothing but one wild, fierce, fitful howl. The cold became intense, and her little feet and hands were fast being benumbed into insensibility.

"It is a fearful change," muttered the child to herself; but still she did not fear, for she had been born in a moorland cottage, and lived all her days among the hardships of the hills. "What will become of the poor sheep?" thought she; but still she scarcely thought of her own danger, for innocence, and youth, and joy, are slow to think of aught evil befalling themselves, and, thinking benignly of all living things, forget their own fear in their pity for others' sorrow. At last she could no longer discern a single mark on the snow either of human steps or of sheep-track, or the foot-print of a wildfowl. Suddenly, too, she felt out of breath and exhausted, and, shedding tears for herself at last, sank down in the snow.

It was now that her heart began to quake with fear. She remembered stories of shepherds lost in the snow; of a mother and a child frozen to death on that very moor; and in a moment she knew that she was to die. Bitterly did the poor child weep; for death was terrible to her, who, though poor, enjoyed the bright little world of youth and innocence. The skies of heaven were dearer than she knew to her; so were the flowers of earth. She had been happy at her work, happy in her sleep, happy in the kirk on Sabbath. A thousand thoughts had the solitary child, and in her own heart was a spring of happiness, pure and undisturbed as any fount that sparkles unseen all the year through, in some quiet nook among the pastoral hills. But now there was to be an end of all this; she was to be frozen to death, and lie there till the thaw might come, and then her father would find her body, and carry it away to be buried in the kirkyard.

The tears were frozen on her cheeks as soon as shed, and scarcely had her little hands strength to clasp themselves together, as the thought of an over-ruling and merciful Lord came across her heart. Then, indeed, the fears of this religious child were calmed, and she heard without terror the plover's wailing cry, and the deep boom of the bittern sounding in the moss. "I will repeat the Lord's Prayer;" and, drawing her plaid more closely around her she whispered beneath its ineffectual cover, "Our Father which art in heaven, hallowed be Thy name; Thy kingdom come; Thy will be done on earth as it is in heaven." Had human aid been within fifty yards, it could have been of no avail: eye could not see her, ear could not hear her in that howling wilderness. But that low prayer was heard in the centre of eternity, and that little sinless child was lying in the snow beneath the all-seeing eye of God.

The maiden, having prayed to her Father in heaven, then thought of her father on earth. Alas, they were not far separated! The father was lying but a short distance from his child; he, too, had sunk down in the drifting snow, after having in less than an hour, exhausted all the strength of fear, pity, hope, despair, and resignation that could rise in a father's heart, blindly seeking to rescue his only child from death, thinking that one desperate exertion might enable them to perish in each other's arms. There they lay within a stone's throw of each other, while a huge snow-drift was every moment piling itself up into a more insurmountable barrier between the dying parent and his dying child.

John Wilson.

NEW YEAR'S EVE.

If you 're waking, call me early, call me early, mother
dear,
For I would see the sun rise upon the glad New Year:
It is the last New Year that I shall ever see;
Then you may lay me low in the mould, and think no
more of me.

To-night I saw the sun set; he set and left behind
The good old year, the dear old time, and all my peace
of mind;
And the New Year's coming up, mother, but I shall
never see
The May upon the blackthorn, the leaf upon the tree.

Last May we made a crown of flowers; we had a merry day!
Beneath the hawthorn on the green they made me Queen of May;
And we danced about the May-pole, and in the hazel copse,
Till Charles's Wain came out above the tall white chimney tops.

There's not a flower on all the hills: the frost is on the pane;
I only wish to live till the snowdrops come again:
I wish the snow would melt, and the sun come out on high;
I long to see a flower so, before the day I die.

The building rook will caw from the windy tall elm tree,
And the tufted plover pipe along the fallow lea;
And the swallow will come back again with summer o'er the wave;
But I shall lie alone, mother, within the mouldering grave.

Upon the chancel casement, and upon that grave of mine,
In the early, early morning, the summer sun will shine,
Before the red cock crows from the farm upon the hill,
When you are warm asleep, mother, and all the world is still.

When the flowers come again, mother, beneath the waning light,
You'll never see me more in the long gray fields at night;
When from the dry dark wold the summer airs blow cool
On the oat-grass, and the sword-grass, and the bulrush in the pool.

You will bury me, my mother, just beneath the haw-
thorn shade,
And you 'll come sometimes and see me where I am
lowly laid:
I shall not forget you, mother; I shall hear you when
you pass,
With your feet above my head, in the long and pleasant
grass.

I have been wild and wayward, but you 'll forgive me
now;
You 'll kiss me, my own mother, upon my cheek and
brow;
Nay—nay—you must not weep, nor let your grief be
wild;
You should not fret for me, mother; you have another
child.

If I can I 'll come again, mother, from out my resting-
place;
Though you will not see me, mother, I shall look upon
your face;
Though I cannot speak a word, I shall hearken what
you say,
And be often, often with you, when you think I 'm far
away.

Good-night, good-night; when I have said good-night
for evermore,
And you see me carried out from the threshold of the door,
Don't let Effie come to see me till my grave be grow-
ing green;
She 'll be a better child to you than I have ever been.

She 'll find my garden-tools upon the granary-floor;
Let her take 'em; they are hers; I shall never garden
more;

But tell her, when I'm gone, to train the rose-bush
that I set
About the parlour-window, and the box of mignonette.

Good-night, sweet mother! call me before the day is
born;
All night I lie awake, but I fall asleep at morn;
But I would see the sun rise upon the glad New Year:
So, if you're waking, call me, call me early, mother dear.

Tennyson.

THE BROOK.

I come from haunts of coot and hern,
I make a sudden sally,
And sparkle out among the fern,
To bicker down a valley.

By thirty hills I hurry down,
Or slip between the ridges;
By twenty thorps, a little town,
And half a hundred bridges.

I chatter over stony ways,
In little sharps and trebles,
I bubble into eddying bays,
I babble on the pebbles.

I chatter, chatter, as I flow
To join the brimming river;
For men may come and men may go,
But I go on for ever.

I wind about, and in and out,
With here a blossom sailing,
And here and there a lusty trout,
And here and there a grayling.

And here and there a foamy flake
  Upon me, as I travel,
With many a silvery water-break
  Above the golden gravel.

I steal by lawns and grassy plots,
  I slide by hazel covers,
I move the sweet forget-me-nots
  That grow for happy lovers.

I murmur under moon and stars
  In brambly wildernesses,
I linger by my shingly bars,
  I loiter round my cresses.

And out again I curve and flow
  To join the brimming river;
For men may come and men may go,
  But I go on for ever.

Tennyson.

THE DISCONTENTED PENDULUM.

Coun′-te-nance	La′-zi-ness	Ha-rangue′
Sur-prise′	Em-ploy′-ment	Sug-gest′-ion
In′-sti-tu-ted	Cal′-cu-la-ting	Il-lus′-trate
Pro-test′-ed	Ex-act′-ly	Mill′-ion
Pen′-du-lum	Mul′-ti-ply	Ex′-e-cute
Sat-is-fac′-tion	Fa-tigue′	Con-sid-er-a′-tion

An old Clock, that had stood for fifty years in a farmer's kitchen without giving its owner any cause of complaint, early one summer's morning, before the family was stirring, suddenly stopped. Upon this the Dial-plate (if we may credit the fable) changed countenance with alarm; the Hands made an ineffectual effort to continue their course, the Wheels remained motionless with surprise; the Weights hung speechless; each member felt disposed to lay the blame on the others. At length the Dial instituted a formal inquiry into the cause of the stoppage; when Hands, Wheels, Weights, with one voice protested their innocence. But now a faint tick was heard below the Pendulum, who thus spoke:—

"I confess myself to be the sole cause of the present stoppage, and am willing for the general satisfaction to assign my reasons. The truth is, that I am tired of ticking."

Upon hearing this the old Clock became so enraged, that it was on the point of *striking*.

"Lazy wire!" exclaimed the Dial-plate.

"As to that," replied the Pendulum, "it is vastly easy for you, Mistress Dial, who have always as everybody knows, set yourself up above me—it is vastly easy for you, I say, to accuse other people of laziness!—you have had nothing to do all your life, but to stare people in the face, and to amuse yourself with watching all that goes on in the kitchen! Think I beseech you, how you would like to be shut up for life in this dark closet, and wag backwards and forwards, year after year, as I do!"

"As to that," said the Dial, "is there not a window in your house on purpose for you to look through?"

"But what," resumed the Pendulum, "although there is a window, I dare not stop, even for an instant, to look out. Besides, I am really weary of my way of life; and, if you please, I'll tell you how I took this disgust at my employment. This morning I happened to be calculating how many times I should have to tick in the course only of the next twenty-four hours—perhaps some of you above there can give me the exact sum?"

The Minute Hand, being *quick at figures*, instantly replied, "Eighty-six thousand four hundred times!"

"Exactly so," replied the Pendulum. "Well, I appeal to you all, if the thought of this was not enough to fatigue one. And when I began to multiply the strokes of one day by those of months and years, really it is no wonder if I felt discouraged at the prospect. So, after a great deal of reasoning and hesitation, thought I to myself, I 'll stop!"

The Dial could scarcely keep its countenance during this harangue; but resuming its gravity at last replied, "Dear Master Pendulum, I am really astonished that such a useful, industrious person as yourself should have been overcome by this suggestion. It is true you have done a great deal of work in your time; so have we all, and are likely to do; and though this may fatigue us to *think* of, the question is will it fatigue us to *do?* Would you now do me the favour to give about half-a-dozen strokes to illustrate my argument?"

The Pendulum complied, and ticked six times at its usual pace.

"Now," resumed the Dial, "was that exertion at all fatiguing to you?"

"Not in the least," replied the Pendulum; "it is not of six strokes that I complain, nor of *sixty*, but of *millions*."

"Very good," replied the Dial; "but recollect that though you may *think* of a million strokes in an instant, you are required to *execute* but one; and that however often you may hereafter have to swing, a moment will always be given you to swing in."

"That consideration staggers me, I confess," said the Pendulum.

"Then I hope," added the Dial-plate, "we shall all immediately return to our duty; for the maids will lie in bed till noon if we stand idling thus."

Upon this the Weights, who had never been accused of *light* conduct, used all their influence in urging him to proceed; when, as with one consent, the Wheels began to turn, the Hands began to move, the Pendulum to wag, and, to its credit, it ticked as loud as ever; while a beam of the rising sun, that streamed through a hole in the kitchen shutter, shining full upon the Dial-plate, made it brighten up as if nothing had been the matter.

When the farmer came down to breakfast, he declared, upon looking at the clock, that his watch had gained half an hour in the night.

Jane Taylor.

THE WRECK OF THE HESPERUS.

It was the schooner Hesperus,
  That sailed the wintry sea;
And the skipper had taken his little daughter,
  To bear him company.

Blue were her eyes as the fairy flax,
  Her cheeks like the dawn of day,
And her bosom white as the hawthorn buds,
  That ope in the month of May.

Down came the storm, and smote amain,
  The vessel in its strength;
She shudder'd and paused, like a frighted steed,
  Then leaped her cable's length.

"Come hither! come hither! my little daughter,
  And do not tremble so,
For I can weather the roughest gale,
  That ever wind did blow."

He wrapped her warm in his seaman's coat
  Against the stinging blast;
He cut a rope from a broken spar,
  And bound her to the mast.

"O father! I hear the church bells ring,
  O say, what may it be?"
"'Tis a fog-bell on a rock-bound coast!"
  And he steered for the open sea.

"O father! I hear the sound of guns,
  O say, what may it be?"
"Some ship in distress, that cannot live
  In such an angry sea!"

"O father! I see a gleaming light,
  O say, what may it be?"
But the father answered never a word—
  A frozen corpse was he.

Then the maiden clasped her hands, and prayed
  That saved she might be;
And she thought of Christ who stilled the wave
  On the lake of Galilee.

And fast through the midnight dark and drear,
  Through the whistling sleet and snow,
Like a sheeted ghost, the vessel swept
  Towards the reef of Norman's Woe.

To the rocks and breakers right ahead
  She drifted, a dreary wreck,
And a whooping billow swept the crew
  Like icicles from her deck.

She struck where the white and fleecy waves
  Looked soft as carded wool,
But the cruel rocks they gored her side,
  Like the horns of an angry bull.

At daybreak on the bleak sea-beach,
  A fisherman stood aghast,
To see the form of a maiden fair,
  Lashed close to a drifting mast.

The salt sea was frozen on her breast,
  The salt tears in her eyes;
And he saw her hair, like the brown sea-weed,
  On the billows fall and rise.

Such was the wreck of the Hesperus,
  In the midnight and the snow!
Christ save us from a death like this,
  On the reef of Norman's Woe!

Longfellow.

"GIVE US THIS DAY OUR DAILY BREAD."

The raven builds her nest on high,
  The loud winds rock her craving brood,
The forest echoes to their cry;
  Who gives the ravens food?

The lion goeth forth to roam
  Wild sandy hills and plains among,
He leaves his little whelps at home:
  Who feeds the lion's young?

God hears the hungry lion's howl,
  He feeds the raven hoarse and grey;
Cares he alone for beast and fowl?
  Are we less dear than they?

Nay, Christian child, kneel down and own
  The hand that feeds thee day by day,
Nor careless with thy lip alone,
  For "all things needful" pray.

God made thy cottage home so dear,
  Gave store enough for frugal fare;
If richer homes have better cheer,
  'Twas God who sent it there.

But better far than garners stored,
  Than bread that honest toil may win,
Than blessings of the laden board,
  The food he gives within.

The lion and the raven die,
  They only ask life's common bread,
Our souls shall live eternally,
  And they too must be fed.

Then not alone for earthly food,
  Teach us with lisping tongue to pray;—
The heavenly meat that makes us good,
  Lord, give us day by day.

C. A. M. W.

THE WHITE SHIP (1120.)

Ret'-i-nue	Eight'-een	Butch'-er
Tri-um'-phant-ly	At-tend'-ance	Be-numb'-ing
Con'-quer	Mer'-ri-ly	Ex-haust'-ed
Har'-bour	Ter-rif'-ic	Brill'-iant
Dis'-so-lute	Whis'-pered	Pres'-ence
De-bauched'	Ag'-o-ny	In-tel'-li-gence

King Henry the First went over to Normandy with his son Prince William, and a great retinue, to have the prince acknowledged as his successor by the Norman nobles, and to contract the promised marriage between him and the daughter of the Count of Anjou. Both these things had been triumphantly done, with great show and rejoicing; and the whole company prepared to embark for home.

On that day, and at that place, there came to the King, Fitz-Stephen, a sea-captain, and said: "My liege, my father served your father all his life upon the sea. He steered the ship with the golden boy upon the prow, in which your father sailed to conquer England. I beseech you to grant me the same office. I have a fair vessel in the harbour here, called the White Ship, manned by fifty sailors of renown. I pray you, sire, to let your servant have the honour of steering you to England!"

"I am sorry, friend," replied the King, "that my vessel is already chosen, and that I cannot therefore sail with the son of the man who served my father. But the prince, with all his company, shall go along with you in the fair White Ship, manned by the fifty sailors of renown."

An hour or two afterwards, the King set sail in the vessel he had chosen, accompanied by other vessels, and sailing all night with a fair and gentle wind, arrived upon the coast of England in the morning. While it was yet night, the people in some of the ships heard a faint wild cry come over the sea and wondered what it was.

Now the prince was a dissolute debauched young man of eighteen, who bore no love to the English, and had declared that when he came to the throne he would yoke them to the plough like oxen. He went aboard the White Ship with one hundred and forty youthful nobles like himself, among whom were eighteen noble ladies of the highest rank. All this gay company, with their servants and the fifty sailors, made three hundred souls.

"Give three casks of wine, Fitz-Stephen," said the prince, "to the fifty sailors of renown. My father the King has sailed out of the harbour. What time is there to make merry here, and yet reach England with the rest?"

"Prince," said Fitz-Stephen, "before morning my fifty and the White Ship shall overtake the swiftest vessel in attendance on your father the King, if we sail at midnight."

Then the prince commanded to make merry; and the sailors drank out the three casks of wine; and the prince and all the noble company danced in the moonlight on the deck of the White Ship.

When, at last, she shot out of the harbour of Barfleur there was not a sober seaman on board. But the sails were all set and the oars all going merrily, Fitz-Stephen at the helm.

The gay young nobles, and the beautiful ladies wrapped up in mantles of various bright colours, to protect them from the cold, talked, laughed, and sang. The prince encouraged the fifty sailors to row harder yet, for the honour of the White Ship.

Crash! a terrific cry broke from three hundred hearts. It was the cry the people in the distant vessels of the King heard faintly on the water. The White Ship had struck upon a rock, and was going down!

Fitz-Stephen hurried the prince into a boat with some few nobles. "Push off," he whispered, "and row to the land. It is not far, and the sea is smooth. The rest of us must die."

But as they rowed away fast from the sinking ship, the prince heard the voice of his sister Marie, the Countess of Perche, calling for help. He never in his life had been so good as he was then. He cried in an agony, "Row back at any risk! I cannot bear to leave her!"

They rowed back. As the prince held out his arms to catch his sister, such numbers leaped in that the boat was overset. And in the same instant the White Ship went down.

Only two men floated. They both clung to the main-yard of the ship, which had broken from the mast, and now supported them. One asked the other who he was. He said, "I am a nobleman, Godfrey by name, the son of Gilbert de l'Aigle, and you?" said he.

"I am Berold, a poor butcher of Rouen," was the answer; then they said together, "Lord be merciful to us both!" and tried to encourage one another, as they drifted in the cold benumbing sea on that unfortunate November night.

By-and-by another man came swimming toward them, whom they knew, when he pushed aside his long wet hair, to be Fitz-Stephen. "Where is the prince?" said he. "Gone! gone!" the two cried together. "Neither he, nor his brother, nor his sister, nor the King's niece, nor her brother, nor any one of the brave three hundred, noble or commoner, except we three, has risen above the water!" Fitz-Stephen, with a ghastly face, cried, "Woe, woe, to me!" and sank to the bottom.

The other two clung to the yard for some hours. At length the young noble said faintly, "I am exhausted, and chilled with the cold, and can hold no longer. Farewell, good friend! God preserve you!" So he dropped and sank, and of all the brilliant crowd, the poor butcher of Rouen alone was saved. In the morning some fishermen saw him floating in his sheepskin coat, and got him into their boat, the sole relater of the dismal tale.

For three days no one dared to carry the intelligence to the King; at length they sent into his presence a little boy, who weeping bitterly, and kneeling at his feet, told him that the White Ship was lost with all on board.

The King fell to the ground like a dead man, and never afterwards was seen to smile.

C. Dickens's Child's Hist. of England.

THE BATTLE OF HOHENLINDEN.

On Linden, when the sun was low,
All bloodless lay the untrodden snow;
And dark as winter was the flow
  Of Iser, rolling rapidly.

But Linden showed another sight,
When the drum beat at dead of night,
Commanding fires of death to light
  The darkness of her scenery.

By torch and trumpet-sound arrayed,
Each horseman drew his battle-blade;
And furious every charger neighed,
  To join the dreadful revelry.

Then shook the hills, with thunder riven;
Then rushed the steed to battle driven;
And volleying like the bolts of heaven,
  Far flashed the red artillery.

But redder still these fires shall glow
On Linden's hills of purpled snow;
And bloodier still shall be the flow
  Of Iser, rolling rapidly.

'Tis morn! but scarce yon level sun
Can pierce the war-cloud rolling dun,
Where furious Frank and fiery Hun
  Shout 'mid their sulphurous canopy.

The combat deepens: On, ye brave!
Who rush to glory, or the grave!
Wave, Munich! all thy banners wave!
  And charge with all thy chivalry!

Few, few shall part where many meet!
The snow shall be their winding-sheet,
And every turf beneath their feet
Shall be a soldier's sepulchre!

Campbell.

THE LIGHTHOUSE.

The rocky ledge runs far into the sea,
And on its outer point, some miles away,
The Lighthouse lifts its massive masonry,
A pillar of fire by night, of cloud by day.

Not one alone; from each projecting cape
And perilous reef along the ocean's verge
Starts into life a dim gigantic shape,
Holding its lantern o'er the restless surge.

Like the great giant Christopher, it stands
Upon the brink of the tempestuous wave,
Wading far out among the rocks and sands,
The night-o'ertaken mariner to save.

And the great ships sail outward and return,
Bending and bowing o'er the billowy swells,
And ever joyful as they see it burn,
They wave their silent welcomes and farewells.

They come forth from the darkness, and their sails
Gleam for a moment only in the blaze,
And eager faces, as the light unveils,
Gaze at the tower, and vanish while they gaze.

"Sail on!" it says, "sail on, ye stately ships!
And with your floating bridge the ocean span,
Be mine to guard this light from all eclipse,
Be yours to bring man nearer unto man!"

Longfellow.

MURDER OF ARTHUR OF BRITTANY (1200).

U-surped'	Pris'-on-er	Shuf'-fling
Sur-prised'	Se'-cret	Ex-e-cu'-tion-er
Va'-ri-ous	Poi'-soned	Mes'-sen-gers
Dun'-geons	Ap-pealed'	Cour-a'-geous-ly
In-hu'-man-ly	E-ter'-nal	Hur'-ried-ly
Neph'-ew	Chafed	En-treat'-ies
Truth'-ful-ness	Sug-gest'-ion	Ob-scure'-ly

Prince Arthur was the right heir to the throne of England, and went to war against his uncle John, who had usurped. Arthur and his army were resting at Mirebeau, a town near Poictiers in France; when one summer night King John, by treachery, got his men into the town, and surprised Arthur's force. He took two hundred of Arthur's knights, and seized the prince himself in bed. The knights were put in heavy irons, and driven away in open carts drawn by bullocks, to various dungeons, where they were most inhumanly treated, and where some of them were starved to death. Prince Arthur was sent to the Castle of Falaise.

One day while he was in prison in that castle, mournfully thinking it strange that one so young should be in so much trouble, and looking out of the small window in the deep dark wall, at the summer sky, and the birds, the door was softly opened, and he saw his uncle the King standing in the shadow of the archway, looking very grim.

"Arthur," said the king, with his wicked eyes more on the stone floor than on his nephew, "will you not trust to the gentleness, and the friendship, and the truthfulness of your loving uncle?"

"I will tell my loving uncle that," replied the boy, "when he does me right. Let him restore to me my kingdom of England, and then come to me and ask the question."

The King looked at him, and then went out. "Keep that boy close prisoner," said he to the warden of the castle.

Then the King took secret council with the worst of his nobles, how the prince was to be got rid of. Some said, put out his eyes and keep him in prison, as Robert of Normandy was kept; others said, have him stabbed; others, have him hanged; others, have him poisoned.

King John sent certain ruffians to Falaise, to blind the boy with red-hot irons—but Arthur so feelingly entreated them, and shed such piteous tears, and so trustfully appealed to Hubert de Bourg, the warden of the castle, who had a love for him, and was an honourable tender man, that Hubert could not bear it. To his eternal honour, he prevented the torture from being performed, and at his own risk sent the savages away.

The chafed and disappointed King bethought himself of the stabbing suggestion next; and with his shuffling manner, and his cruel face, proposed it to one William de Bray. "I am a gentleman, and not an executioner," said William de Bray, and left the presence with disdain.

But it was not difficult for a king to hire a murderer in those days. King John found one for his money, and sent him down to the castle of Falaise. "On what errand dost thou come?" said Hubert to this fellow. "To despatch young Arthur," he returned.

"Go back to him who sent thee," answered Hubert, "and say that I will do it."

King John very well knowing that Hubert would never do it, but that he courageously sent this reply to save the prince or gain time, despatched messengers to convey the young prisoner to the castle of Rouen.

Arthur was soon forced from the good Hubert, of whom he had never stood in greater need than then; carried away by night, and lodged in his new prison, where through his grated window he could hear the deep waters of the river Seine rippling against the stone wall below.

One dark night as he lay sleeping, dreaming perhaps of rescue by those unfortunate gentlemen who were obscurely suffering and dying in his cause, he was roused and bidden by his jailer to come down the staircase to the foot of the tower; he hurriedly dressed himself and obeyed. When they came to the bottom of the winding stairs, and the night air from the river blew upon their faces, the jailer trod upon his torch and put it out. Then Arthur in the darkness was hurriedly drawn into a solitary boat; and in that boat he found his uncle and another man.

He knelt to them, and prayed them not to murder him. Deaf to his entreaties they stabbed him, and sunk his body in the river with heavy stones. When the spring morning broke, the tower door was closed, the boat was gone, the river sparkled on its way, and never more was any trace of the poor boy beheld by mortal eyes.

C. Dickens's Child's Hist. of England.

APPENDIX.

EXERCISES ON WORDS THE SAME IN SOUND, BUT DIFFERENT IN SPELLING AND MEANING.

Adds, ... joins, does add.
adze, ... a cooper's axe.
Ail, ... to be sick.
ale, ... beer; malt liquor.
Air, ... the atmosphere.
Ayr, a town in Scotland.
ere, ... before.
e'er, ... ever.
heir, ... one that inherits.
All, the whole; every one.
awl, an instrument for boring holes in leather.
Alter, ... to change.
altar, that on which offerings are laid.
An, ... a particle.
Ann, or Anne, a woman's name.
Ant, ... an insect.
aunt, a father or mother's sister.
Arc, ... part of a circle.
ark, a chest; the vessel in which Noah was preserved.

Ate, ... did eat.
eight, ... twice four.
Aught, ... any thing.
ought, ... should.
Bad, ... ill, wicked.
bade, ... did bid.
Bail, ... a surety.
bale, a package of goods.
Baize, ... a kind of cloth.
bays, the plural of bay; the laurel-tree.
Bate, ... to lessen
bait, ... a lure for fishes.
Ball, a round body like a globe.
bawl, to cry or shout out.
Bare, ... naked; did bare.
bear, a wild beast; to carry; to suffer; to produce fruit.
Base, the lowest part; low, mean.
bass, ... a part in music.
Bay, ... a colour; a tree; a term in geography.
bey, a Turkish governor.

Be, ... to exist.
bee, ... an insect.
Beach, ... the sea-shore.
beech, ... a timber tree.
Beat, ... to strike.
beet, a kind of vegetable.
Been, ...participle of be.
bean, ... a kind of pulse.
Beer, .. malt liquor.
bier, a frame for carrying the dead to burial.
Beau, a fop; a fashionably dressed person; an admirer.
bow, an instrument to shoot arrows; a kind of knot.
Bell, a hollow sounding vessel. [young lady.
belle, a fashionably dressed
Berry, ... a small fruit.
bury, to inter; to conceal.
Berth, a sleeping place in a ship.
birth, a coming into life.
Bight, a coil or turn of a rope.
bite, to seize with the teeth.
Blew, ... did blow.
blue, ... a colour.
Boar, ...the male swine.
Bore, to annoy; did bear; to make a hole in.
Bough, a branch of a tree.
bow, to bend or stoop.
Brake, ... a thicket.
break, to part by force.
Brays, as an ass; pounds or bruises, as in a mortar.
braze, to solder with brass.
Bread, food made from corn.
bred, ... brought up.
Brews, ... does brew.
bruise, to crush; to hurt.
Broach, a spit; to pierce.
brooch, an ornamental pin.
Brows, ... edges or brinks.
browse, ... to eat shrubs.
Brute, ... a beast.
bruit, ... to noise abroad.
Burrow... rabbit holes.
borough, a corporate town.
But, except, nevertheless.
butt, a cask; a mark to aim at; to thrust with the head.
By, ... near, beside, &c.
buy, ... to purchase.
bye, ... indirectly.
Call, to name; to invoke; to make a short visit.
caul, the network of a wig.
Cane, a reed; a walking stick.
Cain, ... Abel's brother.
Canon, a law or rule in the Church.
cannon,... a great gun.
Cask, ... a barrel.
casque, ... a helmet.
Cast, ... to throw.
caste, a tribe; a class among the Hindoos.

Caws, ... doth caw.
cause, ... a reason.
Ceiling, the inner roof of a room.
sealing, ... as with wax.
Chagrin,... vexation; ill-humour.
shagreen, the skin of a kind of fish, or a kind of leather made rough in imitation of it.
Check, ... to restrain.
cheque, an order for money.
Chair, ... a moveable seat.
char, to work by the day.
Chews, grinds with the teeth.
choose, to select; to prefer.
Chord, the string of a musical instrument.
cord, a string or rope.
Cit, ... a citizen.
sit, ... to be seated.
Cite, to call, or summon.
site, situation or position.
sight, the sense of seeing; the thing seen; a look; a show.
Claws, ... talons.
clause, part of a sentence.
Close, to shut; to finish.
clothes, .. garments; dress.
Coal, ... for burning.
cole, a sort of cabbage.
Coarse,... not fine; gross.
corse, ... a dead body.
course, ...a running; career.
Coarser, more coarse.
courser,... a swift horse.
Coat, ... a part of dress.
cote, a fold for sheep; a cottage.
Coble, ... a fishing boat.
cobble, to mend coarsely; to do clumsily.
Coquette, a flirt.
coquet, to act like a coquette.
Core, the heart or inner part of a tree.
corps, a body of soldiers.
Cousin, a blood relation.
cozen, ... to cheat.
Creek, a narrow bay or inlet.
creak, to make a harsh or grating noise.
Crews, ships' companies.
cruise, to sail up and down.
Dam, the mother; to confine water.
damn, ... to condemn.
Dane, a native of Denmark.
deign, ... to condescend.
Day, the time between sunrise and sunset.
dey, a Moorish governor.
Dear, ... costly; beloved.
deer, ... an animal.
Derbe, an ancient town.
Derby, a town in Derbyshire.
Dew, moisture; the vapour that falls after sunset.
due, ... what is owing.

Die, to expire; a small stamp used in coining.
dye, ... colour; tinge.
Doe, ...the female deer.
dough, ... unbaked paste.
Does, ... female deer.
doze, ... to slumber.
Dun, a dark yellow colour.
done, ... performed.
Dust, earth dried to powder.
dost, ... thou doest.
Dram, a small weight; a glass of spirits.
drachm, ...an ancient coin.
Draft, a bill of exchange.
draught, a drawing; a drink.
Fane, ... a temple.
fain, ... glad; gladly.
feign, ... to dissemble.
Faint, to swoon; weak; languid.
feint, ... a pretence.
Fair, handsome; just or right; a large market.
fare, food; price of passage.
Fate, ... destiny.
fete, ... a festival.
Faun, ... a rural deity.
fawn, a young deer; to flatter meanly.
Feet, parts of the body.
feat, a deed or exploit.
Fellow, a companion; a match.
felloe, the rim of a wheel.

Fillip, a jerk or blow with the finger let go from the thumb.
Philip, ... a man's name.
Flee, ... to run away.
flea, ... an insect.
Flew, ... did fly.
flue, a pipe; a chimney.
Fool, an idiot; a foolish person.
full, ... filled.
Fore, ... in front.
four, ... in number.
Forth, ... forward.
fourth, next after the third.
Foul, ... dirty; nasty.
fowl, ... a bird.
Freeze, to harden as ice.
frieze, coarse woollen cloth.
Furs, skins with soft hair.
furze, ... prickly shrubs.
Gage, ... a pledge.
gauge, to measure a cask, &c.
Gate, a door or entrance.
gait, manner of walking.
Gild, to overlay with leaf-gold.
guild, ... a corporation.
Gilt, adorned with gold.
guilt. crime, wickedness.
Glare, ... dazzling light.
glaire, the white of an egg.
Grate, for holding coals; to rub against a rough surface.
great, ... large, grand.

Grater, a rasp or rough file.
greater, ... larger.
Greece, ... a country.
grease, ... melted fat.
Grieves, laments; causes grief.
greaves, armour for the legs.
Groan, ... to sigh deeply.
grown, increased in growth.
Grocer, a dealer in tea &c
grosser, ... coarser.
Hale, ...strong; healthy.
hail, frozen rain; to wish health to.
Hare, ... an animal.
hair, the covering of the head.
Hall, ... a large room.
haul, ... to pull.
Hart, ... a kind of stag.
heart, ... the seat of life.
Heel, the hind part of the foot. [sound.
heal, to cure; to grow
he'll, ... for *he will*.
Here, ... in this place.
hear, ... to hearken.
Heard, ... did hear.
herd, a drove of cattle.
Hew, ... to cut, to chop.
hue, ... a colour; dye.
Hugh, ... a man's name.
High, ... lofty; tall.
hie, ... to go in haste.
Him, ... that man.
hymn, ... a divine song.
Horde, ... a tribe.
hoard, ... a secret store.
Hole, ... a hollow place.
whole, entire; unbroken.
I, ... myself.
eye, the organ of sight.
I'll ... for *I will*.
isle, ... an island.
aisle, wing or side of a church.
In, ... into.
inn, ... a hotel.
Jam, a conserve of fruit.
jamb, a leg or supporter.
Jessy, a woman's name.
Jesse, ... a man's name.
Jewry, ... Judea.
jury, a set of men *sworn* to give a true verdict.
Key, an instrument for a lock.
quay, ...a wharf or dock.
Kill, to take away life.
Kiln, ... a sort of stove.
Lade, ... to load.
laid, ... placed.
Lane, ... a narrow road.
lain, ... remained.
Lac, ... a kind of gum.
lack, to want; want; need.
Lanch, to cast as a lance.
launch, to push into the sea.
Leaf, part of a plant or book.
lief, ... willingly.

Lea, a meadow; a field.
lee, the sheltered side.
Lead, ... a metal.
led, ... conducted.
Leek, ... a sort of onion.
leak, to let in or out water.
Links, ... plural of link.
lynx, ... a wild beast.
Lo, ... look or behold.
low, not high; humble.
Lone, ... alone.
loan, ... any thing lent.
Made, did make; finished.
maid, a girl or maiden.
Male, the masculine kind.
mail, a bag for letters; armour.
Mane, the hair on the neck of a horse.
main, ... principal; chief.
Mantle, a cloak; a cover.
mantel, the chimney-piece.
Maze, an intricate place.
maize, ... Indian corn.
Marshal, the highest rank in the army; to put in order or arrange.
martial, ... warlike.
Mean, low; to intend or purpose.
mien, air; look; manner.
Meet, to come together; suitable; fit.
mete, to measure.
meat, animal food; any food.

Meter, ... a measurer.
metre, measure; verse.
Mite, a very small insect.
might, strength; power.
Mity, ... full of mites.
mighty, ... very powerful.
Moan, ... to lament.
mown, ... cut down.
Mote, a small particle of dust.
Moat, a deep ditch or trench.
Mewl, to cry as a child.
mule, ... an animal.
Naught, nothing; worthless.
nought, ... not any thing.
Nay, ... no, not.
neigh, ... as a horse.
Nave, the middle part of a wheel.
Knave, ... a rogue.
Need, ... want; necessity.
Knead, ... to work dough.
New, ... fresh; novel.
knew, ... did know.
Night, time of darkness.
Knight, a title of honour.
Not, a word of denial.
knot, ... a tie.
No, ... not so.
know, ... to understand.
None, ... not any.
nun, a religious maid.
Nose, the organ of smell.
knows, ... understands.
Ore, ... unrefined metal
oar, for rowing with
o'er, ... over

Our, ... belonging to us.
hour, ... sixty minutes.
Pale, white; wan; a stake.
pail, a wooden vessel.
Pane, a square of glass.
pain, ache; uneasiness.
Pare, ... to cut thinly.
pair, ... a couple.
pear, ... a fruit.
Pallet, a small mean bed.
palette, a painter's board.
Pall, ... a cloak.
Paul, ... a man's name.
Pause, ... to stop.
paws, ... feet of a beast.
Peace, ... quiet; rest.
piece, a part or portion.
Peak, a point; the top.
pique, a grudge; to give offence.
Peal, ... a ring of bells.
peel, ... rind or skin.
Peer, an equal; a nobleman.
pier, support of a bridge.
Place, ...situation; rank.
plaice, ... a flat fish.
Plain, smooth; a level country.
Plane, a plain surface; a carpenter's tool.
Plate, flat piece of metal, a small shallow dish.
plait, to fold; to braid.
Plum, ... a fruit.
plumb, a leaden weight.
Pole, a long staff; five and and a half yards.
poll, ... the head.
Pore, a minute tube for respiration.
pour, to empty out liquor.
Pray, to ask; to supplicate.
prey, ... spoil; plunder.
Prays, ... does pray.
praise, ... applause.
Pries, examines closely.
prize, ... a reward.
Quire, 24 sheets of paper.
choir, a band of singers.
Rain, water from the clouds.
reign, to rule as a king.
rein, ...part of a bridle.
Raise, to lift up; to excite.
rays, ... beams of light.
raze, to level with the ground.
Rap, to strike quickly.
wrap, ... to roll up.
Read, ... to peruse.
reed, a hollow; jointed stalk.
Read, ... did read.
red, ... a colour.
Reek, ... smoke; vapour.
wreak, to execute vengeance.
Reck, ... to care or heed.
wreck, ruin; to shatter or destroy.
Rest, ... quiet; repose.
wrest, to twist violently from.

Ring, a round or circular figure; to sound a bell.
wring, to twist; to torture.
Rite, a ceremony or observance.
right, ... straight; just.
write, to express by letters.
wright, ... a workman.
Road, ... a way.
rode, ... did ride.
Roe, the female deer; the eggs of a fish.
row, a line; a rank; to propel by oars.
Roam, ... to wander.
Rome, ... a city in Italy.
Rote, ... mere memory.
wrote, ... did write.
Rose, ... a flower.
rows, ... does row.
roes, ... plural of roe.
Rood, the cross; fourth part of an acre.
rude, untaught; rough.
Root, ... part of a plant.
route, road or way; direction.
Ruff, an article of dress.
rough, ...uneven; rugged.
Rye, ... a kind of corn.
wry, ... crooked.
Rung, ... did ring.
wrung, ... twisted.
Sale, selling; the act of selling.
sail, of a ship; a ship.
Sane, ... healthy; sound.
Seine, a river in France.
Scate, a kind of flat fish.
skate, a kind of shoe for sliding on the ice.
Seal, ... a stamp.
ceil, to overlay the inner roof of a building.
Seem, ... to appear.
seam, the line formed by sewing.
Seas, the plural of sea.
sees, ... beholds.
seize, to take by force.
See, to perceive by the eye.
sea, ... the ocean.
Seen, beheld; observed.
scene, a view or prospect.
Sell, to give for a price.
cell, a cellar; a hermit's hut.
Scent, a smell; chase by smell.
sent, ... did send.
cent, for *centum*, a hundred.
Sere or *sear*, dry; withered.
cere, to cover with wax.
Sheer, ... pure; unmixed.
shear, ... to clip or cut.
Sign, a token or symbol.
sine, a line in geometry.
Signet, ... a small seal.
cygnet, ... a young swan.
Sink, ... to descend.
cinque, the French for five.
Skull, ... the head.
scull, a small boat; small oar.

Slight, weak; small; to think little of.
sleight, a dexterous trick.
Slow, ... not swift; dull.
sloe, a small wild plum.
So, thus, in this manner.
sow, ... to scatter seed.
sew, ... to use a needle.
Sole, only; the bottom of the foot.
soul, the spirit; the immortal part of man.
Sore, tender; painful; an injured part.
soar, ... to fly aloft.
Stake, a post; a wager.
steak, a slice of broiled beef.
Stare, to look earnestly.
stair, a step for ascending.
Steal, to take by theft.
steel, iron refined and hardened.
Stile, steps over a fence.
style, manner of writing.
Strait, narrow; a narrow passage.
straight, ... right; direct.
Sum, the whole or amount; to add or cast up.
some, a part of any whole.
Sun, the luminary of the day.
son, ... a male child.
Sweet, pleasing to the senses.
suite, retinue; a set of rooms.
Tacks, ... small nails.
tax, a rate imposed; to charge.
Tale, ... a story.
tail, ... the hinder part.
Tare, a weed among corn.
tear, ... to rend; a rent.
Tier, ... a row, a rank.
tear, water from the eye.
Tease, to annoy; to comb wool.
teas, ... plural of tea.
Teem, to be full of; to pour.
team, a yoke of horses or oxen.
Time, duration; season.
thyme, ... a kind of plant.
There, ... in that place.
their, belonging to them.
Threw, ... did throw.
through, from one end or side to the other.
Throe, extreme pain, agony.
throw, ... to cast, to fling.
Thrown, cast; projected.
throne, a royal seat of state.
Too, ... overmuch; also.
two, twice one; a couple.
Toe, ... of the foot.
tow, the coarse part of flax.
Ton, 20 hundred weight.
tun, a large cask; 252 gallons.
Tray, ... a sort of dish.
trait, ... a feature.

Use, ... to make use of.
ewes, ... female sheep.
Vane, ... a weathercock.
vain, ... empty; false.
vein, ... a blood vessel.
Vale, ... a valley.
vail, ... to yield.
veil, a cover to conceal the face.
Wane, ... to grow less.
wain, ... a waggon.
Waste, to consume uselessly.
waist, the middle part of the human body.
Wait, to stay; to tarry.
weight, heaviness; importance.
Ware, merchandize; goods.
wear, to use; to waste.
Wave, of the sea; to undulate.
waive, to beckon; to defer; to quit.
Way, a road; course; manner.
weigh, to try the weight of anything.
Weather, state of the air.
wether, ... a sheep.
Weak, ... feeble; infirm.
week, the space of seven days.
Won, ... did win.
one, ... in number.
Wood, a forest; timber.
would, past tense of will.
Yoke, a frame for coupling oxen; a couple or pair.
yolk, the yellow part of an egg.
You, the plural of thou.
yew, ... a kind of tree.
ewe, the female sheep.
Your, belonging to you.
ewer, ... a small jug.

THE END.

CPSIA information can be obtained
at www.ICGtesting.com
Printed in the USA
LVHW100028190422
716387LV00030B/237

9 783752 595512